FRIENDS IN NEED

A Paul Stanton Thriller

Chris Darnell

CONTENTS

COPYRIGHT

DEDICATION

I dedicate this novel, with a lifetime's love and thanks, to my Mother, who now will never read it; and to my wife, Nicola Mary Hanney, who left a young Gurkha officer in 1973 but found him again before it was too late.

PART I - KATHMANDU

THE FAVOUR

1

DARK DECEMBER DAYS

THE ATMOSPHERE IN the bar was jolly, but Major Paul Stanton's mood wasn't. Far from it.

'Another drink, saheb?' Politely asked and in broken English.

Paul looked at the young Nepalese barman and smiled tiredly. *'Ma pugchhu, hos,'* he said. *'Ma sathi ko lagi parkanchhu ani yo raksi tikkai chha,'* he pointed at his glass. He was OK for the moment, the night was still young and drinking too much Gurkha rum was a practice he had long forgotten. He *was* also waiting for a friend.

The barman's eyes lit up and he excused himself politely - for the time being. Paul had identified himself as a Gurkhali speaker, albeit a rusty one, a pukka saheb, almost definitely an ex-officer in the Gurkhas and so to be treated as such. Unlike pretty much everyone else in the bar who were trekkers, climbers, travellers and tourists. But at least they looked and acted happy. The bar was humming. And why not? It was the 6th of December, coming up to the year's end and a time for spiritual uplift and family celebration, the advent of a new year and all the hope and exciting challenges it usually brings.

So why did he feel so damned miserable? Paul knew the answer, but it didn't make him feel any better. For him December was a bad month and it would always be the case. It was only three years ago so how could he ever forget that dark December of 1985 when his men had been killed and the lives of three families had been smashed apart forever? Simple; he couldn't. And those death-days in Ireland and Berlin and what he'd had to do? Would he ever forget the final scenes inside the derelict dance hall in the Wall Zone as a devastating storm battered Berlin, and the moment the big German shot him? No, he never would.

For Paul there was no spiritual uplift in such memories; and his family, his widowed mother to be precise, was four thousand six hundred flying miles away, so not close at this moment in time. If anything he should be planning his yearly pilgrimage to Melvilltown to pay respects at the gravesides of his dead soldiers. That's what I should be doing, he thought, rather than using up precious Christmas leave in a bar in Kathmandu, thinking maudlin thoughts, drinking Gurkha rum and waiting for a man.

Except he'd been asked to come. A good friend was in *serious* trouble and needed help. What are good friends for? So get a grip, Stanton, you know perfectly well why you're here.

Paul was sitting on a stool at one end of the long bar and he turned around to look again at the groups of animated trekkers and climbers who formed minor colonies around the packed tables. The Europeans were of all ages, speaking all languages and dressed pretty much in the same way, with functional faded clothing, worn boots and a calculated disregard for how they looked after days in the hills and mountains. The men were bearded and unkempt and the women's hair was long and bleached by the daytime sunlight and the clear air of the higher altitudes. They clustered around their guides, the Sherpas and the darker, more aquiline looking Manangis, listening to their wisdom, or what they believed it to be, and swapping stories. Bowls of food were being devoured and glasses of drink thirstily emptied. It was definitely a place to be happy, he mused, but his morale had sunk to a point where even the atmosphere of Rum Doodle's couldn't make him feel any better.

He was tired and looked it. Although his clothing was also faded and worn he felt out of place, because he wasn't a traveller and he wasn't relaxed. He caught the sound bites of German, French and English in amongst the white noise of the band playing in the opposite corner. The ceiling was low and the room space broken by pillars. Every surface of wall, pillar and ceiling was covered in cardboard yeti feet - the symbol of the bar - on which the members of many of the parties who had come through this landmark bar had signed their names. It was a remarkable testimony, Paul thought. He'd been here once before and looked for and found famous mountaineering names scribbled on some of the yeti feet.

He turned back to the bar and looked at his watch. Where was the man? He signalled for the young barman. '*Malai arko raksi lyaunnus.*' He would have another, after all.

4

'Je, saheb,' the young man responded.

'Been practising the old *kura* then, Paul? Good for you. How are you, mate? Probably a darn sight better than me. No. Wrong of me. Stupid and unthinking. Of course you're not, matey, you couldn't be.' Paul's morale instantly spiked. He hadn't heard the approach of the man amongst the bustling noises of the bar but he'd have recognised the particular verbal art form anywhere and it was just what he had needed to cheer him up. He was about to respond but was not quick enough. The verbal assault rolled on. He smiled to himself.

'Bloody hell,' the man said sympathetically, 'you must be shagged out apart from anything else, coming all this way just to do me a favour. And it's that time of year, isn't it. Miserable for you, old mate.' The man paused, then spoke again, almost reflectively. 'We are a right pair, you and I.'

Paul turned on his stool and looked up at the face of Major Danny Dalloway, ex-of the Kathmandu Rifles, peering down at him in the gloomy light. It was the man he was waiting for. Dalloway was half-smiling and his posture was friendly and familiar, but Paul had the instant feeling of something held-back and restrained in his friend's manner. He made to speak but then sensed Dalloway had more to say, so he waited.

'Eh, *bhai*,' said Dalloway to the barman, and the Nepali flowed off his tongue, 'we are leaving so please bring me one large Gurkha rum, super-quick, and present the bill to my friend here who can pay.' Dalloway turned back to Paul, 'bit of a cheek, I know, Paul, but you must be loaded with all that

5

SAS pay and London allowance you earn. Me? I'm almost as broke as an old tramp. But money's not everything, eh?'

'Hello, Danny. It's very good to see you,' Paul said finally, and he meant it. Paul stood and took the outstretched hand and felt Dalloway's firm grip. He had big hands. He was tall, six feet two at least, so Paul gave him an inch in height, he also gave him several kilos in weight. The last time Paul had seen Dalloway he was as fit and strong as an active thirty-plus year-old, recently retired soldier should have been. He was always big in body, big in attitude and full of life and laughter. Paul studied his friend as Dalloway fussed with the barman and took his drink and saw a subtly different man. Although his eyes were bright and friendly there was the ghost of something uncertain in his look as Dalloway scanned the room, clearly checking or searching for someone or something.

Dalloway swallowed his drink in two huge gulps. That much hadn't changed. Dalloway could drink all right. 'Come on, Paul, pay the man and let's slip our mooring from this place.' He looked over the low-roofed bar and Paul followed his gaze. 'As much as I applaud the youth of Kathmandu in playing rock music, I withdraw my support when they insist on murdering a perfectly brilliant Hendrix number.' Paul laughed softly. Dalloway was right and Paul remembered Dalloway loved classic rock music, as he did. Paul's sub-conscious had probably registered it but he hadn't noticed until now that the three-young Nepalis in the rock band were endlessly jamming the main riffs of Hey Joe. They must have been at it for ten minutes or so. He handed the barman a rupee banknote of appropriate denomination to cover the bill and a good tip.

6

'OK, Danny, I'm in your hands. Lead on.' Paul drained his glass and moved with Dalloway towards the entrance to the bar.

'Don't necessarily want to be in my hands, old mate.' Dalloway stopped in the doorway, turned to him and gripped Paul's arm. 'They're a bit dodgy right now.' The two men went out into the dark, the inference of Dalloway's words hanging in the air between them.

* * *

THE WIND BLEW in a sudden, bitingly cold gust down the street. Paul zipped up his goose down jacket. The nip in the air hit his face and the wind eddies flicked up the detritus of the earlier day that had gathered by the stall fronts and in the gutters by the sides of the street. Paul kicked at some rubbish. Everything was closed up and secured. Rusted, corrugated steel shutters padlocked to the frames of the ramshackle buildings. There was no life and only the light from the moon. The feel of the place was in such contrast to the brightness and activity that had assailed him earlier in the day. Then, it had almost overwhelmed him, as Kathmandu can do to its infrequent visitors, and he had forgotten what it was like. He hadn't been to Nepal for over two years.

'Rup obviously collected you all right then, Paul?' Dalloway's question broke his thoughts as they threaded a path through the dark alleyways. 'It's a bloody nightmare trying to get a taxi at that madhouse airport.'

'He did thanks, Danny. It was kind of you to send him. He seems like a good man.' Dalloway turned to him and nodded his head. The two of them continued on.

Five hours earlier Rup's little battered taxi, one of the hundreds of the baby-Suzukis that clogged the streets, had threaded him and his single grip of clothes from Tribhuvan Airport, through the congested, noisy maze of roads, streets and alleyways into the heart of Thamel and deposited him finally at the Kathmandu Guest House.

Paul hadn't expected to be met, let alone ferried to his lodgings. Having paid his visa fee and crawled out of the airport in search of a taxi, Rup Narayan Chaulagain had intercepted him, holding a scrap of paper proudly in his hand with Paul's name on it, a big, lop-sided, gap-toothed smile on his face and his hand outstretched to take Paul's grip. He spoke English: good English in fact. His words had carried the authenticity Paul needed to go with him: "Dalloway Saheb sends me, Stanton Saheb. I am your designated taxi for the next days." The smile had grown and Paul had gone with him, in the back of his cab, the space so tight that Paul's knees were up under his chin, and the vehicle's suspension so shagged out that every time they hit a pothole Paul felt as though his back had been driven over.

The vehicle was a wreck, but it went; and eventually Paul was deposited somewhere in the labyrinth of Thamel, at the basic but functional room in the guest house Danny Dalloway had booked for him. Paul had negotiated a daily retainer fee with Rup, paid, and agreed he would come back at the eight the next morning. Paul wouldn't need a taxi again that night. Rup told him where he was to meet Dalloway and he could walk there. Rum Doodle's was virtually next door.

Now, as he and Dalloway stalked through the half-lit alleyways, Paul found it hard to register the changes in atmosphere from his earlier arrival. He believed one of the reasons why Kathmandu oftentimes assailed the senses of its visitors was because of the sheer vivid liveliness of the place and the change of pace it forced upon everyone. For a start, you couldn't move quickly and it was hard to breathe clean air. The place was an overwhelming amalgam of congestion and noise. People, smiling and friendly and not pushy, were massed and packed together. Cattle and carts were on the roads, everywhere, in fact, with animals braying and mooing and the sound of whips being cracked and drivers shouting and cajoling ceaselessly.

With all this came smell. Human smells, animal smells, uncleared and heaped-upon-heap-of-trash smells. Parts of the landscape had resembled middens and parts had resembled derelict squatter areas. The broken Wall Zone in Berlin where he'd faced down Krenselauer's hoods and killed Drinkwater was positively modern compared to Kathmandu.

On top of this there was the Kathmandu overlay of unbreathable smog. Fires, factory chimneys burning God-knew-what, and the killing exhaust fumes of hundreds of battered vehicles whose engines were now probably running on home-brewed alcohol made from potato peelings.

The place was an environmental disaster stoking up nicely. But despite all the downsides he had had to admit Kathmandu was colourful, jolly and uplifting, as he had passed all the crowded temples and squares and gazed at the crowded shop-fronts with their hundreds of flags and banners, and at the plethora of street stalls with their vendors trying to coin a meagre existence from the sale of clothing, Buddhist and Hindu artefacts, souvenirs, books, or anything else they had.

It was, as Paul had been reminded, just like the set from *Raiders of the Lost Ark*, or perhaps better, *The Temple of Doom*! So, as Rup had patiently taken all this chaos in his stride and the little car had crawled on its journey, Paul had quietly adjusted his personal karma. After all, he had agreed with himself, if human progress is to be stalled by humanity itself then there is little I can do about it.

But now, at night, it was a different world. Paul had forgotten how unpredictable the power supply could be. Generators were prevalent and most of the main hotels and bars had them, but even so, the ambient light cast over the city was poor. It was mainly from the moon and it made the narrow alleyways and even the main thoroughfares half-dark places where trouble could lurk if it wanted to.

'Isn't there *any* mains electricity in this part of the city?' Paul spoke to Dalloway.

'Yes and no. Sometimes and not always. Stick close to me, Paul.' Paul knew Dalloway was very familiar with the backstreets of this part of Kathmandu. Thamel. One of the hubs of the city. 'And you're right to have brought your cold weather gear. It's bloody cold. People sometimes forget that Nepal gets the seasons just like in the UK. I mean we're not that high in Kathmandu, only four-and-a-half thousand feet, but we're not that far from the Himalayas either, and it's the

Northern Hemisphere, so it's winter. Damn nearly Christmas, for God's sake.' Dalloway had pulled a black woollen hat over his tousle of fair-ish hair and his dark clothing blended him into the poorly lit backdrop of the alleyways. They walked side-by-side and with purpose. Dalloway's head moved constantly, catching Paul's eye occasionally, but actually, Paul decided, he was scanning his arcs and peering into the side streets, looking and being aware all the time. It was almost like being on foot patrol in Belfast.

'What in hell's name's going on, Danny?' Paul looked to Dalloway as he spoke. 'This isn't Northern Ireland. It's not the Falls Road.'

'No, you're right, Paul. But I'm just taking precautions. We're almost there and then I'll fill you in.'

Paul knew Danny Dalloway pretty well. They had been at Sandhurst together, not the same intake, but had known each other there. That was in 1973, fifteen years ago, then they had bumped into each other in Northern Ireland in the seventies and most recently served together in 1983-84 when Paul had done his secondment with the 1st Battalion Kathmandu Rifles, 1 KR, in Brunei. That was before he'd gone to Staff College, before he'd gone back to Ulster, before…before all the things he'd been thinking about earlier: the black events of Dark December 1985.

But this Danny Dalloway was not quite the man he remembered from two years ago when Paul had come out to Nepal as part of his recuperation after Berlin. Dalloway looked normal. 'What's with the clothes, Danny? Not your usual style, surely? Even in winter. Even in Kathmandu?'

11

Paul had always been slightly amazed at Dalloway's dress sense. Out of uniform he'd always been...well, different. There was nothing conventional about Danny Dalloway in his clothes or anything else for that matter. His Gurkhas had loved him. His superiors had been overawed by his ability to deliberately and subtly flout authority and convention. His friends, including Paul, had been frequently appalled by Dalloway's ability to be extreme in both dress and actions. The man liked to be noticed. That was a fair way of describing Major Danny Dalloway. Now he looked like everyone else in Kathmandu, nondescript, tired and scruffy. But clearly on edge.

'Just blending in, matey. Don't want to stand out in a crowd these days. And the last thing I want, or you for that matter, is for anyone other than my friends to see you or think you're anyone other than just another tourist. You've got to be invisible.' Dalloway stopped, looked all around him and then peered into Paul's face. 'Believe me, Paul. This is potentially fucking serious, which is why I asked you to drag yourself away from the home fires back in London. Come on, we're here. This is a safe zone.'

'Safe zone?' Paul looked at Dalloway. The man's expression was deadly earnest. The usual trace of Dalloway mockery and ill-placed humour was missing.

'Yes. Sounds bad, doesn't it? Well it could be. Anyway, let's get out of this bloody cold and get a dram inside us.' They had been walking for about ten minutes. Paul looked up and saw the dim neon sign of the bar. It was lost in amongst the shambles of the buildings in the street, all backed on to each other and encroaching in some architectural way on each other's frontage. The sign was so faint it was hard to spot and wasn't helped by the fact that the first letter of each of the two words were missing. 'There are some people I want you to meet and there are some stories I need to tell you.'

'Lead on, Danny.' The place and the area had the look and feel of the back of beyond. There was no street life at all. The whole situation gave off that faint odour of danger ahead, which Paul realised he had missed and which never failed to rouse either his interest or his fighting instincts. 'I'm your man.' He felt the spark of life returning to his soul. Things are definitely looking up, he thought, and I needed some action to get the blood flowing and dispel the black humours. This was going to be all right after all.

The two of them moved into the small alleyway and climbed up the crumbling stone steps of the *OM & *ERRY bar.

But Paul was wrong. It wouldn't all be all right.

2

THE QUIET AMERICAN

AS THEY MOVED into the bar Paul looked around him, checking the layout and getting a feel for the place. It was what he always did: know your surroundings, assess the people in the place, find the exits. It was standard procedure and deeply ingrained in him from his SAS training.

The lighting was low and he noted there were only hurricane lamps on each table and placed all around the walls and on the bar. It was a medium-sized room, about fifteen metres by fifteen, he reckoned, but not regular in floor layout. The bar was located centrally against the far end, with its racks of bottles and shelves of glasses. Faded advertising slogans were festooned around the walls. The two Nepali barmen were alert, standing behind the bar looking out into the room, searching their domain constantly, noting the state of drinking and watching for any signalled request from their patrons for replenishment. The place was fairly crowded.

'Bit of a change from old Doodle's, eh, Paul,' said Dalloway.

'It is.' Yes, he thought, and it's typical of many roughhouse places I've been in; but Dalloway said this was the safe zone so maybe I'm wrong. 'Looks pretty cosy.' He scanned the room. There were little booths and alcoves housing stained wooden tables, twelve in all, around which were men of all types, sat on dowdy chairs and engaged in earnest conversation, heads low, glasses and bottles of liquor in front of them, smoke curling up from their cigarettes and hanging in a thick layer under the low ceiling. The whole place was a shadow play of flickering movement. The smoke and alcohol fumes, mixed with the human sweat and the reek of little-washed clothing were almost palpable. This was definitely *Raiders of the Lost Ark*.

'Not sure I'd call it cosy, my old mate. Looks a touch rough-and-ready, I know,' said Dalloway as the two of them closed in on a table in the far corner, 'but it's a friendly bar. Owned by some ex-Gurkha mates of mine, so we're OK here. The clientele's all well known. We're fine. We'll be left alone to talk and the boys will give me the heads-up if the *badmash* are spotted in the vicinity and if they try to come in, which they haven't so far during the past few days. They've got other haunts, it seems.'

'Who *are* the enemy, Danny?'

'Tell you in a minute, Paul. Need to get you introduced first. Then brief you in.'

More and more mysterious, thought Paul. 'Well at least there's no band murdering Hendrix,' he replied. 'Doesn't seem like a place for the ladies, either.'

'Not likely! Know these coves, Paul?'

There were four of them and three rose up from their seats as Paul and Dalloway approached. Paul recognised them, but not the one who still sat. The three were of a similar type. Small, dark haired, with weathered Tibetan-Mongolian features split now by broad smiles and showing even white teeth. These men were as tough as teak. Paul knew this for a fact. They had been some of his Gurkhas back in '83 and '84. One in particular had been a close comrade and friend.

Dalloway's right hand moved up and down as he gestured for the men to sit. He drew up one of the vacant chairs, gesturing for Paul to sit in the other. The men formed a close huddle. It seemed Dalloway wanted the meeting to be just another of the several already taking place in this dingy bar and nothing out of the ordinary. Paul remained standing. Who was the stranger? He turned to the sound of Dalloway's voice.

'Thought you might appreciate seeing a few friendly faces, Paul, apart from my ugly old mug, that is. So I rustled up some of your *bahaduris* from the 1st Battalion. The three of them work for me, now, such as that is.' Paul wondered how and why the three Gurkhas were no longer serving and what exactly they were doing for Danny Dalloway. He'd find out very soon, no doubt.

'*Ram ram*, Omparsad, Gopal, Kindraman. *Tapain haru kasto hunu hunchhau?*' Paul favoured the Gurkhas with the honorific form of address and gave them the *Namaste* as he spoke to them and held out his hand to each in turn. They responded by standing briefly, raising their hands in the prayer pose, then shaking his hand, clasping it in both theirs as Gurkhas do to their friends, and gently nodding their heads before sitting down again.

'Oh,' ventured Dalloway. 'This shifty looking rogue is a friend. Goes by the name of Brad Trevelyan.'

An American, possibly, thought Paul, and what sort of friend exactly, and why was he here? Paul looked hard at him for a few seconds. The man said nothing. He was smoking a small cheroot and sipping from a glass of whisky. He had a deeply tanned face, weathered by the outside world, and he wore the nicks and scar-scrapes of an ex-soldier or soldier of fortune. His features were even and made him a good-looking man. Paul couldn't register the colour of the man's eyes, but they were dark, and he wasn't that young either. His mousy-to-greying hair was tied back in a ponytail. Yes, most probably an American, Paul told himself, perhaps living here in some serendipitous cache seeking his version of Hermann Hesse's *Siddhartha*, and now, confusingly, mixed up with Danny Dalloway and the Gurkhas.

'We'll speak in English, Paul,' said Dalloway, 'it's better.' Paul looked at him quizzically and then turned his head back into the room. No one had even noticed them, it seemed. Dalloway explained himself. 'The boys can handle it. It's the lingua franca of the business we're in,' he paused and looked at Trevelyan, 'and Brad doesn't speak the *kura* anyway. So, everyone,' he spoke to the Gurkhas, 'no Nepali.' The three men nodded their heads. 'Might need Swahili, mind,' Dalloway mused as he pushed a clean glass towards Paul and took hold of the bottle of whisky on the table. 'Have a nip, Paul,' he said, 'you're going to need it. And for Christ's sake have a seat,' and Dalloway laughed softly and poured.

Paul decided to get on with things and stretched out a hand to Trevelyan. 'Paul Stanton.' The man half-rose carefully and leaned across the table. He must be just under six feet tall, Paul guessed, judging by his reach, and looked trim and fit looking. His handshake was firm and strong. A good grip. Paul felt the calluses on the palms of Trevelyan's hand. A worker's hand or a soldier's? Definitely the hand of someone who'd been in the field.

'Brad Trevelyan, Major Stanton. Pleased to meet you. Heard a lot about you from Danny here. And from what they've said I believe the Gurkhas think you're kind of special. So I guess you must be good, 'cause I'm mighty impressed by these boys and they don't appear to give praise too lightly.' The American sat back down. 'Anyway, glad to make your acquaintance.' The two men assessed each other for a few seconds.

Paul pulled up his chair and sat next to Dalloway. The American had spoken in a quiet tone and Paul detected what he thought was a slight trace of Southern drawl. He liked the fact the man spoke earnestly, without a hint of sarcasm in what he'd said or how he'd said it. Paul found himself taking to the American. Normally, as his Jocks would have said - and maybe unfairly - Yanks were "full of pish and wind", but this one didn't seem to be. He seemed to be a professional and knew how to act like one.

'Good to see you, saheb.' Omparsad was the first of the Gurkhas to speak and Paul turned towards him and took in the Gurkha's coal-dark eyes and scarred face. Strong memories came flooding back. Omparsad was a warrior of distinction in the Kathmandu Rifles. And he'd always been the most forward, Paul recalled, and was a natural leader. He was also his friend.

'Good to see you, also, Om, and if you feel like it, since Dalloway Saheb is being so covert about everything, you can call me "Paul".' It was an attempt at levity and it worked.

'*Hunchha*, Paul Saheb, I will,' and all of them chuckled and moved about in their chairs recognising Omparsad's deliberate joke.

'Well that worked as I expected it to,' Paul said, and gave out a short burst of laughter. It made him feel good to be with these great people again. He'd missed them, he realised.

'Can't break die-hard habits, now, can we,' Dalloway said. He sipped the whisky and Paul took up the glass of amber nectar Dalloway had poured for him. It tasted very good. The others were having their glasses topped up. He'd have to be careful. The Gurkhas could drink a veteran from any country under the table in hard liquor. They were all smoking. Paul smiled inwardly. Nothing changed. They would still have more wind in their lungs and strength in their legs and chests than anyone else he knew. Omparsad smoked in that typically-Gurkha way of clamping the cigarette between index and second finger and drawing the smoke in through the curled fist held up to his mouth.

A moment of expectancy settled over them all as each drank and some smoked. Paul let his thoughts bed down. He had to be tired from his numbing flight from London via Bangkok but his mind was wired up now and he could put tiredness to one side. There was darkness in the atmosphere.

This might be a safe and friendly bar but the situation was obviously far from it. Paul's sixth sense was alert and searching for the signs of danger he suspected were out there - somewhere. Dalloway's words would give them to him.

'So, down to it.' Dalloway lit a smoke, drew it into his lungs, sipped his whisky, and looked at each of the men and then rested his gaze on Paul. Paul could now see the strain and tension in his friend's face and his mannerisms. He hadn't seen it before - hadn't had the chance - but Dalloway was stretched as tight as a violin string. Mustn't let him snap, Paul said to himself. 'I'm setting up a business, Paul. The others know this, so this is for you, mate.' Dalloway paused. Paul took a sip of his drink and looked around and noted the expectancy on the faces of the Gurkhas. The American was chugging gently at his cheroot and seemed calm.

'As you were telling me two years ago, I assume, although you never told me the detail,' Paul said. He cast his mind back to when he had come out to Nepal, after Berlin and the shooting and after weeks in hospital. He'd come out on his own to start with and then, when she could get away from her desk in MI5, Christina had joined him. They'd had a good time but afterwards…it had gone wrong. 'So exactly what kind of business is it and how have things moved on since you told me about your ideas?' Dalloway had been a rock to him in terms of support and friendship; and his hospitality had been spectacular. He had given Paul great advice, as well. In the evenings they spent together the two men had sipped whisky and Danny Dalloway had told Paul the outline of what he was planning to do, and Paul had been impressed. "I'm setting

20

nineteen eighty-eight as the year in which I really start to do something meaningful and not only help our Gurkha friends but make a bit of money, too." Paul could remember the words and occasion clearly. So when Dalloway called him three days ago and said his business and the interests of the Gurkhas were being threatened, and then added almost casually that there was the possibility of physical threat as well, and he needed a really big favour, Paul had said he'd come.

How could he not? Taking his Christmas leave early was no problem. Paul's personal admin was minimal. He'd called his mother and said he'd try and see her for Christmas but wasn't sure. He'd even cancelled out the possibility of making his December pilgrimage up to Melvilltown in the Scottish Borders. This was more important.

'Good memory, Paul. Yes, and things have really started to move on. It's a private military company business, PMC to the initiated and up-and-coming. Some might call it the mercenary business.'

'But you wouldn't, Danny, would you; because I'm guessing you're planning to use ex-Gurkhas and the Brigade wouldn't be too happy about it if you did and neither would King Birendra and the Rastriya Panchayat, the Government here. Correct?'

'He's got smarts all right, Danny, just as you said,' offered Trevelyan, and leaned back in his chair as if to stretch his body.

'I wouldn't and won't, Paul, as you say, and the reason is because we are not mercenaries. However, it isn't easy to get the message across to those in authority, even with the Brigade of Gurkhas' tacit approval, which I have. But that's not the problem. That is not why I asked you to drag your battle-worn body all the way from London to the High Kingdom here.' Then Dalloway performed one of his sudden changes in conversational direction as he turned and gestured to the bar. One of the barmen came to the table. Paul had been wrong. He was a Gurkha not a Nepali.

'*Je*, saheb?'

'Bhimbahadur, meet Stanton Saheb. He's come from London. He was in 1 KR in nineteen eighty-three and four, but then he went off and did dangerous things in Northern Ireland and Berlin and was badly wounded. He was also out here again in 'eighty-six with the beautiful Dahler Memsaheb. You heard about them, yes, even though they spent most of the time trekking?'

'I did, saheb. Good to meet you, Stanton Saheb.' Paul took the proffered hand.

'Paul, Bhimy was in the Kathmandu Rifles but finished his service two years ago. Now runs this fine establishment with his brother over there, Ganesh. We use this bar a lot and the brothers have been keeping me posted on what's going on.' Dalloway turned back to Bhimbahadur. 'Stanton Saheb is from the SAS, Bhimy, so we have all the protection we need inside,' and Dalloway chuckled at his own poor humour. 'But I do need you to get your boys to check the outside for me again. I cannot be sure we have not been followed here. And then please bring another bottle of whisky and put it on my tab.'

'*Hunchha*, saheb.'

'Sorry your thing with Christina didn't work out, Paul,' said Dalloway. 'None of my business, of course, but we liked her very much. The boys all said she was great.' And she was, thought Paul, as his heart suddenly lurched with painful memory. And she helped save my life. But I wasn't to be her man. The memories were fading but every time they surfaced Paul had to force his thoughts to push them back down into his sub-conscious again. He did it now.

'That's life, as they say,' but he wasn't sure he really meant it. He had moved on, emotionally, but hadn't arrived at anywhere else. There was no woman in his life...once again.

Dalloway picked up the thread of what he was saying and continued as if nothing else had been mentioned. 'No, Paul, it's not about the niceties of "are we mercenaries or can we call ourselves PMCs and thus claim social and business respectability" quote unquote, because apart from anything else I don't believe this business form is sufficiently well understood by anyone yet to make those distinctions. This may be part of the image issue we face, because we're pioneering the way and no one's done quite what we are trying to do here, but it's not the main problem.' Paul interrupted the flow. He wanted to make sure of something.

'But you know about SSL, Security Systems Limited, Danny, don't you? And you know of Management Risks? Surely they and some others have already set the trend?'

'I do, Paul. Both outfits you mention founded by your SAS elders who, as you SAS types always do, seized the moment and have done well.' Dalloway looked at Trevelyan and the Gurkhas, as if about to explain something specifically to them. He continued. 'What these fellows did was clever. Back in UK, oh, five years ago, the dear Mrs Thatcher was just getting into her stride with the privatisation of big state-owned industries. The business marketplace was changing faster than most could imagine. All of a sudden there was Government money available, if you knew where to look for it, which these ex-SAS men did, to found security firms that could provide so-called essential services to overseas corporations with business interests that impacted on Her Majesty's Government. With me, boys?' The Gurkhas nodded their heads. Paul was quietly impressed. The Danny Dalloway he remembered had always been savvy, but had not struck him as someone who could and would read the business runes back in London quite so cleverly and then apply the principles to setting up a business in Nepal. This was a new man he was listening to.

'But?'

'Yes, but whilst they may have helped the governments around the world to coin the phrase PMC, and helped to create a line of business that was not instantly referred to as mercenary, these companies are not yet doing what I plan to do, and of course they don't have the draw on the Gurkha manpower we have here.'

'So what's got you fussed, Danny? What's causing that note of caution in what you're telling me?'

Dalloway took his time answering. He looked at the Gurkhas and at the American, as if seeking their unspoken agreement for what he was about to say next.

'Believe it or not, Hungarians.'

3

A DEADLY BUSINESS

IT WAS NOT quite the response Paul had expected. ''Fraid you'll have to be a little more explicit, Danny.'

'Yes, Hungarians.' Dalloway looked at the American. 'Brad here has been helping me, unofficially mind, with some information gathering about what these Hungarians I'm talking about are really up to. It's one of the reasons why he's here tonight. So, Brad, please explain to Paul the context in which we find ourselves.'

'Sure, Danny, sure I will.' Trevelyan stubbed out the remnants of his cheroot and leaned forward over the table, almost conspiratorially. Paul saw the colour of the man's eyes in the glow from the hurricane lamp and they were brown as a mudflat and his face told his age at anything between thirty-five and forty. 'Paul, you will, I am definitely sure, be aware of what is going on in Europe right now. Especially the East.' Paul let the rhetorical question hang in the air and waited for Trevelyan to continue. The man's demeanour had changed. He was lucid, cogent and clear speaking. His Southern drawl lessened. He became business-like in speech and manner, what Paul would have called an East Coast American business manner, which was rather disappointing in a way. He thought he liked the laconic and lazy-seeming American. 'You remember what happened back in June last year, in Berlin?'

Paul re-synched his thoughts. Berlin in June 1987? 'I do. Your esteemed President Reagan stood in front of the Brandenburg Gate and at the end of his speech challenged Gorbachev to "tear down this wall", as I recall he said it.' Paul was not an Eastern European watcher, as they called it in the Intelligence world. He had been working in a staff appointment in the Ministry of Defence for the past eighteen months but his desk was focused on equipping UK's Special Forces. Those who gave him his jobs had put him in a posting where he could regain his strength, jog in to Whitehall from his flat in Pimlico every morning and back at day's end, take his allotted allocation of leave and not have to subject himself to the rigours of exercises and operations. And it had worked. He had been passed fully fit again. 'I always wondered if Regan's speechwriters stole the line from Pink Floyd's *The Wall*,' he continued. Dalloway chuckled at this. Trevelyan didn't seem to pick up on Paul's intended irony.

'You might be interested to know that Mr Reagan's speechwriters had trouble with the line. Didn't want to include it since it might test the relations that were coalescing with Gorbachev at the time, and be interpreted as too provocative. But anyway, the President kind of liked it and so he kept it in.'

'Good for him. It's bound to become a classic. Just like JFK's botched "Ich bin ein Berliner" back in 'sixty-three.' And this time Dalloway laughed out loud but Trevelyan kept his face neutral. No sense of irony, thought Paul. But who is he? Ex-CIA? He felt he ought to say something conciliatory. 'Well, you never know, Brad, his words might yet prove to be visionary.'

'That's for sure, by my reading of things and from what I hear from back home, Stateside,' said the American. The words reinforced Paul's forming view that the man was quite possibly ex-CIA and despite his new-age hippy appearance was still connected into his information networks somehow. He had to be. Why else would Dalloway be using him?

Trevelyan sat back and lit another cheroot. He hadn't finished all of what he was about to say, that was obvious, but Bhimbahadur had stolen up to the table and was speaking softly into Dalloway's ear. When he'd finished, the Gurkha went back to the bar. His message changed the tempo of the conversation.

'Bhimy tells me that he's heard some strangers, and I don't mean tourists, have been seen going into the Maya Cocktail Bar, which is not a million miles from here. Most likely the Hungarians I've been talking about. Last thing we all want is for them to find us together in here. We should finish up pretty soon and anyway I need to get back up to headquarters before too long.' He turned to Paul. 'Back up to the Hotel Khumjung, Paul, up on the northern Ring Road at Maharajgunj. It's where I stay and have established a small admin base for the business.' Dalloway paused and smoked his cigarette. Trevelyan's briefing seemed to have been forgotten.

'Do you all stay there?' Paul asked Omparsad.

'*Hoina*, saheb. We come in from outside Kathmandu.' The Gurkha chuckled and dragged on his smoke. 'It is less money for living than Kathmandu prices. And Dalloway Saheb's *paisa pugdaina, mero bichar ma.*' The other two Gurkhas chuckled in unison and smiled.

'Of course my money isn't enough,' Dalloway retorted, 'you cheeky blighter, Omparsad! Especially since I've taken a girl on board, as well. Young woman, to be accurate,' Dalloway said to Paul, who raised an eyebrow in question. 'She controls the back office, or whatever the hell it's supposed to be called. I had to. You now how famously shambolic my admin is, Paul. And she's a stunner. Not my type if I'm being truthful, which is probably the way it should be inside a business. Hopefully you'll meet her.' Paul said nothing but looked at Trevelyan, who just quietly shook his head. What did *that* mean, Paul asked himself. Dalloway answered the question. 'No she's strictly business.' Dalloway chuckled and had a drink.

'Is she out of town?' Paul's curiosity had been piqued.

'Yes, in the Chitwan National Park for a few days break. I met her watching Elephant Polo down there last year. She was on the rebound from a pretty disastrous business relationship.' Dalloway seemed to hesitate for a second, possibly realising that what he'd just said could be tempting fate. 'She'll be back the day after tomorrow, in fact, so you should catch her.'

'Why is she here?' Paul asked.

'Because the business was some sort of ceramics import-export set up, shipping stuff from all over the East and she was in China when her partner - business and personal - did a runner with all the loot and one of the local women. She ended up here. She's an outdoors type and goes by the name of Nikki Walker-Haig. It's a bit of a mouthful so I call her double scotch, which she hates. Despite her tag she's as English as we are. You two might get on,' and he winked at Paul

'Never been anywhere near elephants, Danny, so I doubt it.'

'Well, that's as may be. But on a serious note she needs to be kept out of whatever might happen, Paul.'

'OK. I don't have a clue what that means, but you'll tell me, I'm sure.' Paul looked at his watch. It was eight p.m. He realised he was starving. 'I know you're in a bit of a hurry, but any chance of some *bhat*, Danny? Eat and talk at the same time? I'm starving.'

Before Dalloway could respond, Omparsad said, 'I will bring you some, saheb. Gopal *bhai*, you come with me, Kindraman, stay here and listen. You need to know more about what is going on.' Paul looked at the Gurkhas. So he wasn't the only relative newcomer to the situation. The two Gurkhas moved away towards the bar and Omparsad signalled to Bhimbahadur.

'You spotted it, Paul,' said Dalloway, 'Om's my eyes and ears and he's a natural leader as you know well. He and Gopal were the first to join this venture, and then Kindraman came on board. There are also a total of fifteen ex-Gurkhas who will definitely join us and have the right qualifications and motivations. They're all living fairly local to Kathmandu. I can't afford to bring them onto the books just yet. And then there are the many other Gurkhas in the hills who've already shown an interest in working for me. So it's a fledgling organisation, so far, but with much promise,' and here Dalloway paused in personal reflection for a second before going on. 'Yes, great promise, which is why the Hungarians have to be dealt with.' Paul resisted the temptation to speak. Dalloway turned to Trevelyan. 'Christ, Brad, my apologies, old mate, I got distracted by Bhimy's info. And before I forget,' he said to Paul, 'I'll show you the ropes of it all tomorrow, in daylight. Go on, please, Brad,' Dalloway said, 'tell Paul more about why we think the Hungarians are here.'

Trevelyan lit another cheroot, twisted his face as its pungent smoke hit his eye, and carried on with his briefing. 'So, Paul, the forces of democracy are taking their first bold steps in the East of Europe. Capitalism has been unleashed. I'm no expert but our State Department analysts see the Wall coming down anytime soon. Your Iron Lady, along with Gorby there and our President, are gonna change the face of modern Western history, so all the academics are saying.'

'Just who are you, Mr Trevelyan?' Paul needed some clarity about the apparent dichotomies in the American.

Dalloway tut-tutted good-naturedly. 'Yes, he's a bit of an odd one, I agree. Go on Brad, tell the man, and then for God's sake finish the story because I have to get a weave on.'

'I'm ex-CIA, Major Stanton, and I mean ex-, -ex, really out of the Langley business. I'm an undesirable as far as the forces of covert US Intelligence are concerned. Why do you think I'd be up here in this town just underneath the roof of the world if I wasn't an undesirable? I'm a nothing, just a drop out.'

'But not *so* dropped out, Brad, otherwise Danny here wouldn't have found you somehow.'

'Well, I guess you have a point there, Mister.' Trevelyan smiled and Dalloway laughed and winked at Kindraman. Even if Trevelyan didn't have a sense of irony he did seem to have a sense of humour, Paul said to himself. Yes, I think I quite like this mysterious, quiet American.

'So what are you really doing, scouting opportunities for Uncle Sam or spying? Perhaps both,' Paul said, tongue-in-cheek, and all of them laughed.

'Well spoken, Paul. God you bring cheer to my heart in these worrisome times. I'm glad you're here. And it's not just because your ugly mug with that bent nose of yours makes me feel handsome, either!' Dalloway drank a huge gulp from his glass and turned in Paul's direction. Trevelyan was unfazed. Kindraman had a great big beaming smile on his round face, watching all the character plays. He was clearly enjoying seeing the sahebs making fun of each other. 'No, Brad's not part of the business, Paul, and just as well he isn't. As far as prying eyes are concerned he's just another traveller. We've kept Brad and the business strictly separate.'

'What happened between you and the CIA?' Paul sidestepped Dalloway's comment and spoke to the American. He wanted to know more about him.

'That, my British friend, is a story for another day, if you don't mind. Back to the Hungarians.' At which point Omparsad and Gopal arrived at the table followed closely by

Bhimbahadur. They brought plates of pork fried in ghee, a large bowl of vegetables, the same of rice, dhal and a dish of chillies. Paul waited until the Gurkhas had sat and all three had helped themselves to some food and then ploughed in. It was delicious.

'Not eating, Danny, Brad?'

'No, thanks. I'll get mine up at HQ, at the hotel, and Brad doesn't eat. Just feeds himself on tar and whisky.'

Paul raised his eyebrows in mock surprise and chewed gratefully. God, it *was* good food and hot, too. 'You were saying, Brad?'

'Hungary is leading the way, so it would appear, in breaking the yoke of its Soviet-dominated puppet masters.' Paul stopped eating and looked thoughtfully at the American. He was an educated man. Well he would be, wouldn't he, as an ex-Langley operative. 'And as a result its criminal entrepreneurs, black marketeers, mafia, if you want to be accurate, scent an opportunity to get ahead in the beckoning game of new capitalism.'

'Here? In Nepal?' Paul was trying to correlate what Trevelyan was saying with what he knew and read about in the intelligence digests he occasionally saw and the weekly black ops briefs circulated to him from Special Forces Headquarters in Duke of York's Barracks in London.

'Yes. Not many at present, but the spider webs of the old world black business are increasing. There are hints coming out of Budapest that Hungary will open its border with Austria, and if that happens the writing will literally be on the wall. East Germany will go. And when the Wall comes tumbling down, which it will if those boys back in Langley have their predictions correct, then the first Russians to break out will be the gangsters. Then we'll be in for something, you bet your boots on it.' Trevelyan stubbed out his cheroot and took a drink. Paul pushed his plate to one side. He'd bolted his meal. He looked at the Gurkhas. They were still quietly and carefully eating, watching him. He caught Omparsad's eye and the Gurkha smiled and just tilted his head in that inimitable Gurkha way.

Dalloway spoke. 'As Brad said, Paul, we've got the advance party of the Eastern thugs here. We've identified three hoods and we've got names for two of them. One is called Benko and one's called Karas. We don't know the name of the third. They're all nasty pieces of work. They seem to think they can waltz into Kathmandu and ignore business protocol. So far they've got some of the more disreputable Manangis to do foot-soldier work for them: beat people up a bit, damage their goods, that sort of stuff. And they're smart enough to stay off the radar screen of the police, who at best are ineffectual and most likely are, in my view, unaware of the phenomenon of evolving organised crime. As you know, Kathmandu tends to self-regulate itself. This is a peaceful place. Karma rules, eh.'

'They've followed the drug trails,' said Trevelyan, 'and not surprisingly it's led them to Kathmandu.'

'They're also in Thailand, Afghanistan, all the usual places,' continued Dalloway. 'That's what Brad means when he talks about the spider webs. Just follow where the drugs come from and where they end up and all of a sudden we've got old world gangsterism, with its ugly Slavic face pushing its bad intent into our peaceful little world up here. As I told you, the Nepalis seem not to have latched on to the threat and where it might lead. This is the advance party we're talking about. Just wait until the main body arrives.'

'But it's not drugs that's our concern, here.' The American spoke again. The reason why he was here was gradually becoming clearer, Paul thought. He knew Danny Dalloway wouldn't be doing anything that involved drugs. Not with Gurkhas. 'At the moment it's protection rackets. These would-be mobsters from Hungary see themselves taking a sizeable share of other peoples' businesses without doing a damned thing except putting the squeeze on those concerned. It's good old New York or London gangster stuff. That's the problem Danny faces, as I understand it.'

'They're testing the water, so to speak,' said Dalloway, 'and because they've been relatively successful in coercing a number of the smaller guest house owners, stall owners and bar owners, all peace-loving Nepalis, I should add, they've decided to look for targets in other areas. God knows how they found me or even knew about me, except that the whole bloody city is raddled with tittle-tattle, of course, but they waltzed into the Hotel Khumjung ten days ago and told me how much I was going to pay them! I thought they were taking the piss. I mean, for goodness sake, I don't even have a bloody business yet! But could I get that message across to them? Could I hell. They said they'd heard I was a "bizniz" man from London, Christ, that's how they said it. Spoke quite good English, too. What a joke. So I must have money, they said, and they would have their share of it or they would burn down the building. It was like a scene out of a B gangster movie and would have been hysterically funny if it wasn't so deadly serious. Imagine how public, burning down the old hotel would be. Imagine how public it would get trying to stop them. It would be the Gunfight at the OK Corral all over, except in High Town Kathmandu and not Tombstone.'

'Does make you laugh, though Danny, just thinking about it,' said Trevelyan.

'Well, in another time and other situation, maybe. Christ, I'm only renting some living accommodation, a storeroom and a briefing and admin area with an office. It's a bloody Kathmandu hotel!' Dalloway took a drink and lit another cigarette. 'The really crazy thing is that these Slavs have absolutely no idea who or what they're threatening; the Gurkhas would make mincemeat of them as soon as I gave the word.' Paul looked at Omparsad, whose inscrutable expression said nothing; but Paul could have sworn he read a message in the Gurkhas eyes: *we need to take some action*, or was he just being dramatic? Dalloway went on. 'They have, in an old-world, Eastern European way, utterly misjudged the situation but have put me in an arm-lock despite it.' Dalloway dragged smoke into his lungs deeply and sat back. 'If you can make heads or tails of any of that, Paul.' He leant forward again. 'And they've put a deadline on my acceptance.'

Paul registered the last, ominous comment. 'So it's accept their terms or take the consequences.'

'Yes.' Dalloway's voice was hushed. The Gurkhas stopped eating and looked up expectantly. Trevelyan quietly smoked and looked at Paul with a steady eye and a calm expression on his face. He's going to be an asset, this man, thought Paul, in whatever it is I've let myself in for.

'What's the deadline, Danny and what are the terms?'

'The deadline's now, well in two days, but that's as good as now. The terms are unacceptable, as I've said.'

'Yes, I can see that,' said Paul.

But Dalloway was on a roll. 'Even if I wanted to I couldn't give these hoods what they're asking. As I've said, we've hardly got an infrastructure or support operation established yet. Fact is we have no tangible assets, no wealth. So whilst they think we have business and cash, we don't. It's all *potential*; but try telling that to old-world Slavs. I can't be seen even to be talking to these hoods. Their reputation as gangsters will grow if they are allowed to stay here, and I will be tarred by their particular brush and that will be curtains for the business. Furthermore, I will have spectacularly reneged on some privileged friendships and some carefully nurtured business opportunities.' Dalloway looked seriously at the three Gurkhas and said, 'What's more, I'll have let down these three boys of ours and all those that still want to join us. It's Catch-22. I can't give them what they want, even if I wanted to, which I certainly don't and won't. Get my drift, Paul?'

'I get your drift, Danny, but I'm still trying to grab grass in the wind for some of the detail. So help me more. You talked about certain "privileged friendships". What exactly do you mean?'

Dalloway continued. 'What I'm talking about, Paul, is that there's politics involved in what we're doing. Politics that have effects outside this little Kingdom. It's one of the reasons why I looked for someone like Brad to help me understand the context. Whilst there are UK interests involved there are also US issues. The sceptics might say my business plan is based on false promises but I know it isn't, *provided*,' and Dalloway placed the emphasis on the word and dragged on his smoke, 'I keep the faith.' He exhaled and paused. 'I've got the key contacts made and I'm starting to get the people,' and Dalloway indicated the Gurkhas, 'to do something really special and really new. I'll be taking the PMC concept in a different direction to anyone else and with a stroke or two of good fortune, before anyone else. It's a great opportunity.'

'What's the faith you spoke of? Why do you need me?' There was an important piece in all this that Paul needed to be sure of. 'Come on, Danny, three or four Hungarians? As you said, they'd be no problem for the Gurkhas. So you're telling me you and the boys here can't flush them out and deal with them? I find that not credible.' Paul looked at Omparsad but the Gurkha's expression remained unfathomable. I'm missing something subtle here, Paul thought. 'So it's to do with perception, then, is it?'

'It is, Paul,' said Dalloway, 'that's exactly what it's about. My nascent business and anyone who helps me,' and here Dalloway gestured to the three Gurkhas and waved his arm over towards the bar where Bhimbahadur and his brother stood watching all that was going on, 'cannot be seen to be tainted, touched, tarnished in any way by what these gangsters want. Emphasis on the word *seen*, Paul.' Dalloway looked sorrowfully at Paul. 'So somehow these bloody Hungarians have to be made to leave me alone, and I mean totally alone. Sorry to be so dramatic, but I did talk to Brad about it quite a lot before I contacted you. I needed to make sure I wasn't just being a wet fart about everything.' Paul looked at the American who raised an eyebrow in agreement. 'Whatever happens to them has to be one hundred per cent deniable. To not happen, as far as I'm concerned.' Paul nodded his head slowly as he started to think through what Dalloway was saying. 'And you're the one person, friend, I know who can do such things. You'll need help, obviously, but the boys can give you that, I'm sure, and we can still ensure their required anonymity. After all, our Gurkhas are masters at blending in with the locals, they come in from out of town and they're not yet officially registered with the authorities as part of the business personnel.'

'What about Brad, here?' Paul asked. He had a feeling he would need help from the American.

'As I said,' and Dalloway looked mischievously at the American, 'Brad's just another amongst the thousands of new-age hippies that flood Kathmandu and exist somewhere and somehow within its limits.' And Dalloway laughed gently at his wit, as if it would lighten the weight of the atmosphere that had descended over the small group.

Paul understood now. He had very recent experience of Eastern Bloc gangsters. Dalloway knew what had happened in Berlin. And he owed Danny Dalloway, who was now, unashamedly calling in the favour. Fair enough, Paul said to himself, that's how it goes.

'I get it, Danny,' Paul said. 'You and yours have to be squeaky clean, totally accountable in everything you do.'

'I do. So thanks, mate. It's a lot to ask, I know, but...'

Paul cut him off. 'I need all the information, Danny. I need to see your operation as well. And I need to see the enemy.'

'You do. All of the above. I'll show you around tomorrow, Paul, as I said, and introduce you to some other key people.' Dalloway looked at his watch. 'Then Omparsad can brief you in on the Hungarians and where they've been operating. But right now I have to get back up to the Khumjung. It's an early start tomorrow for me and you should get some kip, mate. We've got a breather of thirty-six hours tops. The boys will see you back to the guesthouse. Get Rup to bring you up to the hotel. He knows where it is. Make it zero eight hundred hours. The Gurkhas will be in at that time.'

4

THE EARLY STRIKE

THERE WERE SLEDGE hammers at work inside Paul's dream and the men using them were shouting. It was too real to be ignored. He struggled to get to grips with where he was and what was happening. He was in the Kathmandu Guest House. OK, got it. Now what's that bloody noise? He forced his eyelids open. There was just the hint of grey inside the room. Well that's progress, Paul thought, daylight's coming. There had been no electricity when he'd got back to his room. To make it all even more black and unwelcoming his room had been freezing. Paul had piled on every blanket and piece of clothing he could find and then wormed his way into the narrow bed. It was barely long enough to take his six feet one inches of height, so he'd bent his knees, put the Hungarians out of his mind, thought good thoughts and sunk instantly into a deep pit of sleep. Now he couldn't dig himself out of it and he had to because of the noise and the shouting.

'Who is it?' He was finally making progress.

'Stanton Saheb, it is Raj, your landlord, and Omparsad is with me. You must open up, saheb. Please! It is most urgent.'

'Coming.' Paul had a sixth sense when it came to danger and had a bad feeling about this early morning rousting. The thirty-six hours Dalloway had talked about had not existed. That had to be something to do with it. Damn and bloody blast him for getting that crucial factor wrong. He had the feeling that he was now going to be in catch up mode against the bastard Hungarians.

He got to the door. The room was bitterly cold. His watch told him it was just after 7 a.m. He unlocked it and stood in front of the anxious faces of Raj, the owner of the guesthouse, and Omparsad, who looked like he hadn't been to bed. 'Is it Dalloway Saheb?' He was sure it was.

'Yes, saheb,' said Omparsad. 'He is in the Bir Hospital.'

Paul was already dressing. 'He's alive?'

'Yes, saheb.'

'Tell me, quickly, Om. Was it the *dushman* we were talking about, the Hungarians?'

'Yes, saheb. And Trevelyan Saheb is with him.'

'How do we get to the hospital?'

Raj answered. 'Rup, your taxi driver, is outside, saheb. Omparsad brought him. I have tea for you downstairs, saheb. You will need some and it will only take a minute to drink.'

'I will, Raj, and thank you. Give me two minutes then I'll be with you.' The two men left and Paul quickly finished getting dressed, made a basic ablution and then stuffed some clothing into his small daysack. It was cold now and they were going to a hospital. He'd be inside and then outside in the warm winter daytime. He needed some different clothing. He

41

had no weapons of any description, but that would be a problem for later. He also had no clear notion of what he was going to do but he was going to do *something*, that was for definite. He locked his room and took the flights of stairs down to the lobby.

They were drinking tea. Paul nodded hello to Rup, who looked sad-faced. He hadn't been a Gurkha soldier so the notion of violence would be alien to him. Raj handed Paul a tall cup of thick, sweet milk tea, just how he had liked it when he'd been in the Kathmandu Rifles. He sipped gingerly and felt the energy flood into his system. He looked at Omparsad's face and saw the tension and tiredness there. The man's been up most of the night, I'm guessing. Where was he staying? He must have been relatively close to be here now. It will hurt him deeply that his Saheb has been attacked. Well, bad luck, you bastard Hungarians. Now you've set the game rules, and that's fine. Paul's mind was racing.

'How is Dalloway Saheb hurt, Om?'

'It is his eye, saheb. I have not seen him but that is what Trevelyan Saheb wrote in his message. He sent Rup to come for me. Trevelyan Saheb's instructions were for me to find you and bring you to the Bir Hospital. He said Dalloway Saheb was in good hands. Those were his words.'

'You did well, Om, and so did you, Rup.'

As he drank quickly Paul thought about how Omparsad would be feeling. In early 1984 Paul had been given command of B Company 1 KR for his last six months before he had to leave for the Army's Staff College. The Battalion was in Brunei as a result of the cycle of postings for Gurkha

42

battalions: 2 KR was in UK and 3 KR in Hong Kong. Paul had specifically asked not to go to 2 KR. He'd seen more than enough of Aldershot, Sennybridge Training Area and the Brecon Beacons during his years in the Scottish Infantry and the SAS. He'd been to Brunei for his SAS jungle training in 1979, but had seen nothing of the country other than the jungle, which he'd not exactly liked. But this time he'd be with Gurkhas so all would be well.

In Brunei he'd met Omparsad, who was the Company Sergeant Major of B Company. The two of them became true friends. Paul had seen some great warriors in his time, Jocks and SAS soldiers, but Omparsad was amongst the finest, toughest and bravest. He had been awarded the Military Medal in Borneo in 1964, as a young rifleman, during the Undeclared War that was called Confrontation. In a totally fearless act during a fighting withdrawal, Omparsad had taken on significant numbers of Indonesian soldiers and killed eight of them and then bailed out, fighting all the way until he got back inside his platoon's perimeter. Because the Gurkhas love the symbols of bravery and prize those of their number who have them, Paul had had to tell them the story of his action in the Falklands, for which he'd been awarded the Military Cross, and been wounded as well. He and Omparsad had enjoyed a special relationship bred out of mutual respect and from being genuinely comfortable in each other's company.

'We should leave now, saheb.' Omparsad's gently spoken words brought him back to the present.

'I'm ready. Thank you, Raj. Lead on, Rup.' Paul hefted up his daysack and followed the other two outside.

Ordinarily, he thought, someone like Omparsad would have been commissioned. After the talk last night Paul believed he had worked out the reason why he hadn't and why he was here on this grey morning, as part of a fledgling manpower-based business.

The Falklands War in 1982 had delayed the cuts in the John Nott Defence Review, but it hadn't cancelled them. By late 1985 early 1986 the Gurkhas were faced with the need to lose a battalion. So 3 KR had been disbanded and selected senior Gurkhas from all the battalions had been offered a small compensation package to retire. Danny Dalloway had left on a British Officer's package. Dalloway had told Paul this when they'd met up again in Nepal two years ago. He'd been one of the first to leave the Gurkhas and he'd come straight to Kathmandu. And I bet, Paul mused, he persuaded Omparsad and maybe the other two as well, to take their early pensions and come and work for him. Dalloway would be paying them out of his own pocket, Paul was sure of it, until he got a contract, which was what this was all about.

So Omparsad's loyalty would be rock solid. There would be vengeance for what has happened. Paul felt a sense of grim satisfaction at the thought of it. He had needed action and it looked very much like he was going to get it. But he knew from bitter experience it would not be straightforward.

* * *

PAUL HAD BEEN impressed with the quiet, clean efficiency of the Bir Hospital. It had looked dull and a touch neglected from the outside, a concrete-fronted, slab-faced building sitting in the heart of the city and at odds with the ancient and colourful surrounds of the Durbar Square. At this early hour it had not taken Rup long to drive them down from Thamel. It was very close.

On arriving at the hospital Brad had not tried to tell the story, but had simply taken Paul and Omparsad to a small private office and introduced them to a Nepalese man dressed in the white coat of a doctor who was sitting at the desk and who looked exhausted. 'This is the guy to give you the details, Paul, he'll tell you the worst,' said the American.

Paul looked at the Nepali who stood up and faced him. His eyes were bloodshot with fatigue and his expression was earnest and concerned. 'I'm Santa Gurung, a surgeon, and an old friend of Danny Dalloway's.' Paul and Omparsad introduced themselves. The man spoke impeccable English.

Paul had a vital question to ask before any discussion. 'My apologies for being so abrupt, Santa, but can you please help in keeping my, our, visits here to Danny as low profile as possible? I know it won't be totally possible but anything you can do will help Danny in the future.'

'I can. Danny will not be attended in his room whilst you are here. Only by me. But I cannot keep his injury secret.'

'No, of course you can't. But if you are a true friend of his, as you say, then you will need to help me in something else as well. You know the cause of his injury, because Brad here and Danny himself will have talked to you. Am I right?'

'Yes. They have both told me something; but not much.'

'This particular cause of his injuries must not be put on the official records. Do you understand?' The Nepalese surgeon nodded his head cautiously. Paul went on. 'I don't know what else might have caused an injury similar to this one of Danny's, but it cannot be recorded on the hospital's records as street violence or a beating or anything like that. The Police cannot be involved. If they are then we will have done more damage to Danny than physical damage.' Paul left the words hanging. Santa Gurung was a smart man. He understood.

'It will be accidental blunt trauma damage. Danny brought himself into the hospital in a taxi. I will discuss it later with Danny and I can advise him on how it might have been caused, as you say.' The doctor paused. 'But as you will see, it will not be easy to explain such damage. A very bad fall onto or into contact with a sharp, cutting surface or object might just about do it.'

'Thank you, Santa. That is really important for the future. Now, please, what's the prognosis.'

'He has suffered penetration and blunt trauma of the left eye. There is rupturing and contusion, the cornea has been cut and the eye globe has been badly damaged. In addition his eye socket is broken.'

Paul looked at the other two. Their faces were deadpan. He was trying to imagine the pain involved and the consequences for Dalloway's future. 'Christ,' was all he could say.

Santa Gurung said, 'From what Danny told us, whoever did this used a big knife. The left side of his face has been slashed from his forehead down across his cheekbone. It's a deep cut.' The surgeon paused, and Paul could see he was holding back the anger he felt at how his friend had been brutally injured. But he was far from finished. 'Then the men smashed his eyeball with the handle of the knife and fractured the bone structure of the eye's orbit, rupturing the fatty tissue and muscle as well. The blunt force of the weapon's handle has crushed the cornea and lens, almost certainly beyond future surgical repair.'

'Christ,' Paul said again. His mind was reeling. Omparsad grunted quietly and his body moved as if experiencing some of the pain.

'The eyeball is still in place but is next to useless. I have given him a CT scan and X-ray, but I am not a qualified ophthalmologist. However, even I can see the retina has been massively traumatised. It has become detached from the inside wall of the eye and the optic nerve looks torn.'

'Which means he probably won't see, from that eye, Santa. Is that right?' Paul asked.

'It does.' The Nepali surgeon went on. 'I've had him in care now for some hours and have followed the procedural processes for such injuries. He is stabilised and the eyeball has been fully irrigated to clear out any possible infection. As I said, I've examined and assessed both the visual pathways and the eye globe integrity; but the specialist will need to make his own conclusions and that will not be until much later today.'

'What are the next steps?' Paul asked.

'I shall keep him in hospital for the time being. He will be kept under a mix of antibiotics and painkillers for the next two days when the specialist will re-examine him and set out a treatment and surgical plan for his eye repair. This will take a number of days and it will start sometime much later, when Danny is ready for it.'

* * *

THAT CONVERSATION HAD been thirty minutes ago. Now Paul was sitting in the chair next to Dalloway's bed and his thoughts were racing. He was impressed with Danny Dalloway's indomitable spirit. But he was not impressed with the injuries to his friend. It reinforced the resolution he had made that certain people were going to pay for what had been done; and judging by the look on Trevelyan's face and knowing how Omparsad and the other Gurkhas would feel, Paul was quite certain the Hungarians had no concept of what they had started here. I hope they think they're protected, Paul said to himself, because I'm going to tear down *their* walls and make them wish they'd never left Hungary.

Brad Trevelyan was behind him looking out of the window at the now bright morning. It was warming up and Paul was glad he'd stuffed a lighter weight shirt in his daysack. Omparsad was standing quietly in the other corner. Paul turned his head and glanced at him. Omparsad wore a blank look on his tired face. Paul could only imagine what thoughts were churning in the man's mind behind that give-nothing-away exterior. Most likely undiluted fury, Paul thought, just like me. He cautioned himself: patience, get the facts, identify the enemy, build the plan with those who can help you and then get payback.

'How do I look, Paul?'

'Pretty ropey, Danny, sorry. You know me, not one to hide the truth, even from good friends.' Paul said it with what he hoped was a touch of levity, but his friend looked truly shocking. 'And it's going to get worse before it gets better, if I know anything.'

'Hah, hah…ow! That hurt,' said Dalloway. 'Not good at giving much on the sympathy or optimism fronts are you.'

'Shouldn't laugh if I was you.' Paul winced inside.

'Impressive surgeon, eh, Paul? Santa says I'll have to wear a patch.'

'Most impressive, Danny. And it will suit you. You always wanted to appear piratical to the ladies, didn't you?' Dalloway looked utterly wasted.

'Yes, mate; but not like this! And the Hungarians told me it was a warning, apparently. Bastards! What does that mean, I ask you.'

It means, Paul thought, that they have to be stopped because they're stupid and unwise enough to do something else. 'At least the hospital's tidied you up a bit, Danny, fit to take visitors.' It was lame humour.

'Aren't they darlings, eh, those lovely Nepalese nurses. Did you see them?' No we didn't, Paul thought, and he gently shook his head and smiled a sympathetic half-smile as he looked at his friend. The whole left side of Dalloway's face was carefully covered in a soft lint pad, held in place with tape positioned so as to avoid the eye socket and the line of the knife wound, which had been cleaned and stitched. Santa and his team had carefully shaved the hair off the left side of his scalp so the tape would stick. 'Yes, mate, wonderful nurses and brilliant Santa Gurung, eh. Like all of you, true friends in a crisis. He's a Royal Nepalese Police surgeon, can you believe it? What a great man. His wife's a nurse, too. Lucky I know the family. I asked the hospital staff to get hold of him when the taxi dropped me off. Naughty of me, really. Christ, you should have seen the blood all over the place. Just as well I had a handkerchief. Don't suppose we'll find the taxi driver again so I can pay him some damage money.'

Paul knew the morphine and other drugs and all the tiredness and shock were having their effect. The bursts of Dalloway's speech and the randomly connected thoughts were sure signs. 'We'll find him, Danny. I'm sure Rup will know his fellow drivers. He's waiting outside for us, so we can ask him later.' Paul stood up and looked over to Trevelyan. The man nodded and moved away from the window, gesturing to Omparsad. 'We'll give you a break, Danny. The pain must be pretty bad. I think there's some stuff that Brad and Omparsad and I need to talk about. So we'll check with Santa on the way out and then come back later to see how you're doing. OK?'

'*Tik chha*, Paul. Sounds good. I could do with some kip, as it happens.'

5

A FRIEND IN NEED

WHEN THEY LEFT the Bir, Paul told Rup to stay with the taxi, parked up where he was by the hospital, and gave the little Nepali some more money to buy food and drink. 'Wait for me, Rup.' The man nodded gravely. 'I will find you shortly and then you can take me to some places and give me some information.' Paul looked at his watch. It was already ten o'clock. His energy was flagging. 'Om,' Paul turned to the Gurkha, 'before I do anything more I must eat. Some sweet milk tea and hot fresh bread rolls. Do you know a place? Where we can talk also?'

'Follow me, saheb.'

Within minutes Omparsad found what Paul was looking for, a small street vendor pitched on the pavement of one of the side streets leading off the Kantipath Road, where they could sit on dirty white plastic chairs and look out across at the mêlée of tourists and local traders swarming in towards Durbar Square. The three of them took the chairs, pulled them into a tight group and sat. Omparsad then went to the vendor and gave him instructions. The vendor's boy went hurtling off down the street and was soon back clutching a large brown paper bag. He gave it to his father who put it on the tray he had ready with the tea, and carried it over to them. Paul paid and thanked the man, who then left the three strangers to their business.

Paul bit into a hot roll and felt instantly better in body but his soul was still in a dark and sorrowful place. 'Tell me what happened, please, Brad, because I'm sure you agree that I have a serious plan to make. But first, I need to know everything that you know.'

'I'll tell you what I know, buddy, but there's some stuff that Danny's been dealing with directly.'

'To do with the Hungarians?'

'No, more on the politics side of things. You know what I mean?'

'No, but I'll get to that later.'

'Yeh, I guess you will, 'cause the truth is, I don't fully know. You gotta remember I'm only an advisor to Danny, and I have to use even that word cautiously. As the man said last night, this business of his is very contained.' The American paused and chewed his bread. Paul felt a sense of mild exasperation. He looked at Omparsad. The Gurkha's expression was neutral but he knew the man and knew he would say to him let the American say what he will. Re-tune your karma, Paul.

'OK. Tell me what you can.'

'I got the call from the hospital, from Santa, at zero five-thirty hours. Danny gave him my number. I don't stay in the hotel with Danny, as you heard. I have a separate place and I like it like that. Santa told me the basics of Danny's injuries. I went straight to the hotel to get hold of Danny's contact list. I called Rup in. Then I wrote a note for Omparsad here, gave it to Rup and told him to go get Omparsad and take him down to fetch you. The rest you know.' Omparsad nodded his head in acknowledgement of what the American had said. 'Then I high-tailed it down here to the Bir. Santa had had Danny in treatment since zero two-thirty hours.'

'So it was three hours before you got the news?'

'Yeh. Three hours. That's why Santa said he'd had some time to do the initial assessment on Danny and get the repairs underway,' and here Trevelyan's voice softened. Then he continued and there was a sudden fire in his tone. 'But as we now know he is never gonna be fully repaired.'

'What do you know about the incident?'

'He says he was ambushed on his way back to the Khumjung Hotel. It was some low-life Manangis, river-rafting guides. Scum. He heard them talking as they took him away. Where to exactly, he doesn't know. They had him hooded and kept him in a woodshed for some hours until the Hungarians arrived. Then the Slavs interrogated him. It seems those guys were not satisfied with the answers he had given them about the money they wanted, because they started to go to work on him. Santa didn't tell you about that. Those Hungarians beat up his feet some, with short wooden planks, Danny said. It's a form of old Arab torture that looks to break up the small bones in the soles of the feet. But they're obviously stupid because they left his boots on, which gave him some protection. It'll take a few days to get the swelling down but he'll walk just fine, so the Doc says.'

Paul breathed in deeply and looked at Omparsad. The Gurkha had finished eating his bread and was smoking and watching, still in posture. Taking it all in. This was all new to him, too.

'So when Danny didn't say what those bastards wanted him to say they cut him and broke up his eye socket,' Trevelyan continued. 'The Hungarians dumped him somewhere on the ring road. A taxi found him. It was his one stroke of luck, and Danny had the presence of mind get himself to the Bir and tell the duty doctor and nurses to get hold of Santa Gurung at his home. He even had the man's number; and that man has performed goddammed miracles in those hours.'

'He has.' Paul looked at the American. 'Then Santa called you?'

Trevelyan lit a smoke and drew in the bitter smoke. 'He did. Danny had my contact.'

'Well then, by hurting Danny, these gangsters have just unleashed a shit-storm on themselves. They have no idea. None at all. They have crossed the line, as they say.'

'That they have,' said Trevelyan, and Omparsad nodded his agreement.

'Now,' Paul said to Trevelyan, 'just tell me some more about the reasons why you guys can't take these stupid Slavs out of the game yourselves. Talk to me, please.'

'My own view, from what Danny's told me? It's all about the politics of this business deal he's after. Danny's somehow managed to get backing from certain people inside your Government back in London for his PMC proposals. But

54

they've put caveats on what he can do, so he tells me. He also tells me your Prime Minister has even been briefed in. What do you make of that?'

Paul knew the Prime Minister personally. He was one of her special SAS boys, as she occasionally referred to the elite men of 22 SAS. What he had done in Ireland and Berlin had had her full cognisance. Nothing anyone said about Mrs Thatcher would have surprised him.

'Nothing,' Paul said. 'Anything more? What caveats? What do you mean?'

'He's got some sort of a framework proposal to provide security, using the Gurkhas, to major corporate customers operating with government sanction in southern Africa. And I don't just mean British Government approval, here. It might have cause and effect on the US State Department as well and other governments in the Region, like Zimbabwe.' And now Paul was surprised. 'Which is why Danny boy came looking for an American and found me,' Trevelyan finished.

'Did you know about this, Om?'

'A little, saheb. Not the detail. But Dalloway Saheb has been working hard for almost one year to make this proposal. He has even been back to London. It is why some of us took the redundancy offer, to come and work with him. Now there are only three of us, but there will be many. As Dalloway Saheb said, we have fifteen close by, waiting to be signed on. But there are many others. Gopal and Kindraman have been building the list of ex-*sipahis*, ex-soldiers, who are still fit and want to be soldiers again. They have been travelling back into the hills and the villages and we have over one hundred and fifty names already. Dalloway Saheb has been talking with the officials here to make a proper recruitment process for it and to build salary and pension plans. He also has to find the equipment and weapons and that will need Panchayat approval.' Paul was impressed. Now the bigger picture was really beginning to take shape. He'd put it all together later. With Dalloway.

'Any more?' Paul asked Trevelyan.

'So our Danny boy found me and asked me to do some investigation, some information gathering, as he told you yesterday. He's a persuasive man and he sells his thoughts with real conviction. I was living a peaceful existence, until he found me and blew on those embers I did not believe I still had, and fanned them into a pretty strong flame.' Nice metaphor, Paul thought. So Trevelyan had really dropped out. Well he'd find out the American's story another time. 'And now the man I've been trying to help is broken and half-blind and I'm not sure how I can help him. The Gurkhas here are great but I don't really know them too well and I sure don't speak their language. So I guess it's up to you, Paul. His old friend and from what I hear pretty damned good black ops man. Ruthless, even, so he once described you.'

'I'm not ruthless. I'm fair. What were you in the CIA, research, management or a field operative?'

'I had my fair share of action but it wasn't why I first joined the Agency.'

'OK. Then that definitely makes me team leader for what we're going to do next. Agreed.'

'Agreed.'

'Good, because it was a rhetorical question anyway.' Trevelyan chuckled. Paul went on. 'But we're going to be invisible. As Danny said, we don't exist as far as his business is concerned. It will be an in-and-out operation and we'll leave no traces, nothing that can be tied back to Danny and the business. Are you OK with that?'

'I am, sir, I surely am.' Paul looked at Omparsad whose face was beaming and whose head was slowly nodding in agreement and excitement.

'You have certain skills and obvious contacts and this is Nepal. So can you get hold of a handgun and ammunition?' Paul asked Trevelyan.

'I can.'

'Then get me one. Nine millimetre preferably. It needs a suppressor and the weapon must be untraceable to the local police. I don't need many bullets. I'm not going to start a war, just execute a surgical hit. It's up to you whether or not you get yourself armed. I'm leaving Kathmandu once this is done but you have to stay. It's your choice.' Paul wasn't about to ask the American how he was going to get a firearm. He was ex-CIA, he had a network and this was Kathmandu where anything and everything was possible. He'd said he could do it. That was good enough. He turned to Omparsad. 'Om, I need some more of the Gurkhas. Those from outside Kathmandu and who can disappear back outside the city after we have finished. Can you fix this?'

'Yes, saheb. How many?'

'To be confirmed, but maybe all of them, all fifteen. For surveillance, tracking and clean-up. Good men with experience, who are not well known inside Kathmandu.'

'*Hunchha*, saheb.'

'You and the boys will not need firearms, OK?'

'No, saheb, we will not, we have other weapons.' The kukri, Paul acknowledged. Perfect.

'Can you find out where these *badmash* have their base? And do we have a safe place where we can meet and prepare?'

'Yes, saheb, I will put the boys onto it as soon as we have finished and we will get the information you need. And I know a place. It will be the back room of Bhimy's bar.'

'Good. Thank you. We will meet back at the hospital at fourteen hundred hours. I'm going to get some money from the bank, do a little shopping and explore this city. I'll use Rup.' He wasn't giving the others a choice. He needed the little Nepalese more than they did. Paul got up from his chair and faced them. He had been thinking furiously and made up his mind. Speed was critical. The Hungarians would not be expecting a strike back, and even if they were, not immediately. 'Brad, I'll need the weapon for tonight and it needs to have been cleaned and checked over. Om, we need the information on the Hungarians also by tonight. We will gather and plan at Bhimbahadur's bar later this evening. The Gurkhas will need to have been given a warning order and be ready to move at very short notice. Can we do all this in the time?'

The American and the Gurkha nodded their heads.

'Om, warn Gopal, Kindraman and the others that it will be a night operation.' Paul looked earnestly at the two men. They didn't need to be told but he'd say it anyway. 'Security is critical. No leaks. We're going to do this quickly.'

The American and the Gurkha nodded their heads once again. Good, thought Paul, we can make this work. I can pull this plan together.

He left them and went to get Rup, who would take him to a bank and then help him carry out a reconnaissance for the idea that was forming in his head. Yes, he thought, as he waved a little farewell to the others, the bloody Hungarians had it coming to them. He was going to pay them back in kind, many times over, and all of them.

And he would talk to Danny Dalloway before the others got back.

6

A BUSINESS PLAN

PAUL GOT TO the Bir Hospital at twelve-thirty. The place was quiet and filled with calm. He let himself into Dalloway's room. It was empty of nurses. Not surprisingly Danny Dalloway was looking worse than when Paul had seen him earlier, but he seemed alert. Paul could see how swollen and bruised the left side of Dalloway's face had become. There was a glorious mélange of colours showing through in deep purples and reds, spreading out from underneath his lint bandage pad. His right eye was bloodshot from tiredness, stress and the lingering effects of morphine.

'Feeling any better, Danny?'

'Like shit, mate. And the bloody morphine's wearing off and Santa's fucked off and the lovely nurses won't give me any more until they say so. So yes, Paul, it hurts like some Hungarian bastard has sliced my face off. And I'd forgotten about my bloody feet. The fuckers beat me with planks, the bastards. The old nurses are pretty though, bless them. What a thing, eh!'

He was going to be all right, thought Paul, because he has the spirit and attitude. But also because I'm going to put it right. 'Sorry if I'm a little short on sympathy, Danny, but the others will be here in just over an hour and there are things you have to tell me about, if I'm going to help you further.'

'Bloody hell, Paul, don't say that. You're the only one who can do this.'

'Then tell me anything else I might need to know, so I can do what I'm good at and get home for Christmas. Leave out the detail about the plan you have with Omparsad, Gopal and Kindraman, how you're establishing a database of the Gurkhas who have come back on early pension or are already here but want to work for you, and who will provide you with your manpower, in due course.'

'I see Brad and Om have brought you up to speed, then.'

'To a certain extent, yes, but how you're setting up the admin for your business is not what you brought me out here to show me or to ask me to help you with. Brad left gaps in what he told me. So you tell me. The real reason *why* you need me.'

'Yeh, Brad would have left stuff out, mate. I haven't told him all the nitty-gritty. Not by a long way. He's not yet in the business, if you get my meaning. Not sure he's ever going to be, actually.'

'Fine. I understand. Then tell me. Fill in the gaps. Tell me more about the politics, Danny, so I can judge whether or not what we do will keep you in the clear. Christ, man, you're asking a lot here, you know.'

'I am, and I'm sorry.'

61

'Don't get all sentimental now, Danny. It's OK. What the Hungarians have done has them going beyond the pale as far as I'm concerned. But I need to hear it from you as well. I have a plan to make, no time, and assets that cannot be seen to be involved, so I must know what the possible fallout might be before I go ahead and do anything.' Paul sat down in the bedside chair. 'And tell me a bit more about the American.'

'Wow. Quite a shopping list, mate.' Dalloway seemed to relax into his mountain of pillows and his bloodshot eye roved around the room before focusing on Paul. 'In answer to your main question. It was quite simple, my old SAS mate, I hoped you'd somehow get rid of the fuckers, but now I hope you kill the bastards!' Paul screwed his face into a wry grimace. 'OK, Paul, the rest, and it's the abridged version but I promise there's nothing of significance left out. I don't have the energy or the mental alertness for the full version, anyway.'

'The short story will do, Danny. Go for it. Start with the politics.'

'The politics. Well then. It's southern Africa, Paul, Mozambique to be precise. I don't know how au fait you are with what's going on in that part of the world but the short answer is a bloody civil war. Since 1977 the Frelimo governing party has been slaughtering the Renamo opposition and vice versa, and both factions in pursuit of their ideological and political goals have been slaughtering those in the middle, namely the local people. It's an example of a classic and catastrophic collapse of a functioning society on the departure of the colonial power, the Portuguese. What's new, eh, Paul? The whole region tells the same story. Malawi, Tanzania,

Zambia, and Zimbabwe will come next.' Once more Paul found himself being quietly impressed with Dalloway's grasp of the geo-politics in question, especially as he must be feeling like shit, he thought. 'But here we come to it. In amongst all this fighting and political positioning there is massive wealth, wealth to be exploited by the countries themselves, and by the grasping capitalist global organisations who work with the countries and who somehow can carve out a piece of the action.'

'And you're working with one of them.'

'Got it in one; well, hoping to work with one of them, if the fucking Hungarians don't completely bugger it up. The fact is, as I told you last night, they're a total distraction.'

'Which company?'

'Heard of MozLon?' Paul shook his head. 'Owned by a lovable, bastard rogue called Reggie Hanlon, Sir Reggie Hanlon, who's big in favour with our own Mrs T, from what I hear.' Dalloway took a pause. 'Help me with a drink of water, Paul, please.' Paul reached for the plastic glass of water and put it in his friend's hand. Dalloway sipped gratefully. 'MozLon's developed and exploited platinum in South Africa and owns the oil pipeline from Beira in Mozambique to Zimbabwe, but the company has many other interests. Hanlon's a modern day Cecil Rhodes. Yes, that's a good way of describing him, because in amongst the pursuit of wealth he's been playing a hand in regional politics.'

'In what way?'

63

'Shuttle diplomacy. Bringing the spokespersons of the regional leaders together to broker, facilitate, call it what you like, the peace process in Mozambique.'

'Why?' Although Paul knew instinctively the answer to his question.

'Because he's a meddling, power-mad, crazy bastard, perhaps? No, that description might be too slanderous. Because he wants to expand his business in Mozambique. He wants to develop certain areas for large-scale agricultural farming. To put the land in question to growing exportable vegetable products. He'll farm them cheaply, in mass volume and export them worldwide and make huge profits. He'll pay over-the-odds for the land rights, but it'll still be dirt-cheap to him. Then he'll pay off the Frelimo Government, employ local people, rejuvenate shipping and transportation and at the same time, through his shuttle diplomacy, help Frelimo secure a sustainable and profitable peace with Renamo that is acceptable in the eyes of the regional leaders and the global powers with an interest in Southern Africa. Which are, principally, the UK, the US and Portugal, and of course Zimbabwe and South Africa.' He sighed. 'Phew. Not bad, eh, for a man with a butchered face and one eye.'

'Damn good, Danny. Thanks. And your new company will provide physical security to these so-called farms.'

'That's the plan, Paul. That's the plan.' Dalloway looked wearied by his efforts. Paul looked at his watch. He had half an hour. 'MozLon knows only too well how vulnerable the farming enterprises will be. Isolated, in the open, civilian workers; you can imagine how tempting they'll be to rebel elements in Renamo and any other anti-government guerrilla bands in the border areas to attack, rape and pillage. Fact is, mate, the details have yet to be worked out,' Dalloway continued, 'but I happen to know Hanlon's Head of Security. An ex-Met Police Fraud Squad gentleman by the name of Fred Etherington. I met him in Hong Kong when he was on secondment to the Hong Kong Police to help them out with their corruption investigations. We became drinking buddies. He contacted me and said something might be up, so I flew back to London.'

'And he put some special conditions on any prospective deal, I'm guessing, and the Hungarians have the potential to scupper it.'

'He did and they do. Etherington's been honest with me. He has Sir Reggie's ear and has sold the concept of private security forces to him, based on using Gurkhas, the most trustworthy soldiers in the world, famed for their ferocity and fighting skills, and politically acceptable in the context of any non-mercenary type of operation. It's beautiful and I've got the head-start on it, because I'm here and I have the loyalty of our Gurkha boys.' He sighed. 'And, as I said, I've got the approval in principle from both the Brigade of Gurkhas and the Panchayat. Then along come the bloody Hungarians who are only after protection money.'

'Has Etherington been out here? Does he have any notion of these local issues you're dealing with? The Hungarians?'

'Not fucking likely, Paul! No he doesn't. And no, he hasn't been out here. Yet. But I know for sure, 'cause he made it crystal clear when I met him in London, that not only does my operation have to be officially sanctioned here in Nepal, it has to be one hundred per cent corruption-free. My words, not his.'

'Which makes sense,' said Paul, 'given his background with anti-corruption and Sir Reggie Hanlon's tightrope-walking in regional politics and big business. As well as his connections to Her Majesty's Government in London.'

'Spot on, Paul. I mean Etherington's a smart bloke. He knows how the world works, especially in places like this and obviously Africa. He knows that bribery, corruption and backhanders are the usual currencies of business, along with the Yankee Dollar, of course. But he was really adamant about the terms, the possible terms, I should say, because as we speak I'm trying to put the proposal together, with all the guarantees asked for. It's one of the reasons why I took on Nikki, since she's good at the paperwork and she's business smart.'

'And so the Hungarians have to go.' Paul just about had all he needed to know. Well nearly, but Dalloway spoke again.

'Any sniff at all that there is corruption or illegality involved, or third parties, then I'm dead in the water and MozLon will go to another PMC organisation. It's a bastard. As I said, the Hungarians gave me two days to agree to their terms; but the fact that they hit me last night indicates they're in a hurry. And I have to produce the business proposal to MozLon, with the required diligences, in two week's time. And then there's the small matter of my own financial wellbeing. If I don't land this deal, Paul, then I'm busted, wrecked. I've been keeping the three Gurkhas on a retainer, paying them out of my own pocket and I've been funding the trips into the hills to find the other Gurkhas who might want to join me.'

'That's what I thought, Danny. You're a good man.'

'No I'm not. I'm a fucking high risk disaster area; but I tell you something, Paul, I'm going to make this enterprise happen, if only for the Gurkhas.' Dalloway took a deep breath. 'And I've had to pay Nikki something to keep her on board. Then there are all the legal fees required to register the business here.'

'What about Trevelyan?'

'No, I'm not paying Brad and he hasn't asked for anything. He's a good man, that one. But add it all up and I'm just about squeezed dry.'

'You'll get the deal, Danny. And you're not giving the Hungarians anything.' Dalloway looked at him. Paul needed two more pieces of information. 'How established are they?'

'As I said last night. Advance party, really. There are definitely three of them.' Dalloway looked intently at Paul, as if silently querying if the targets were manageable. 'The leader is called Tamas Benko and his number two is Virag Karas. It was Benko who cut me. He's an evil-looking fucker. Typical Slav. No humour and no scruples. Cuts you and beats the living daylights out of you with a smile on his pig-ugly face.' Dalloway shivered at the memory. He went on. 'There was the third man with Benko and Karas. I don't know his name. The bastards laughed when they threw me out in the street.'

'What about the Manangis who ambushed you?'

'They're low-life. They act as guides for river rafting trips but they also have a reputation for being available to do dirty work. I heard them speaking and it was just a job to them. I knew they were somehow involved on the fringes because Bhimbahadur had told me. They'll disappear, Paul, once the Hungarians go. They'll melt back into the Kathmandu scene and won't have existed.' Dalloway paused and looked at Paul earnestly. His face was a shocker. 'They left when the Hungarians arrived. They weren't anywhere to be seen later on. Problem is, mate, I don't have a clue where it took place. Because afterwards the bastard Hungarians hooded me again and drove me around in some rust bucket, probably round in circles, for all I know, and then chucked me out of the car on the Ring Road.'

'Thanks, Danny, and don't worry. I'll find these bastards. I've got Om working on that now. In fact he and Brad are due back here any moment and there's one more thing I need to know before they get here.'

'Fire away, my old mate, I'm just about shot with talking anyway.'

'Tell me about Brad.'

'Straightforward, really. Etherington told me that ideally I needed an American in my operational structure somewhere. Nod and a wink stuff, he said, someone who could get information from people close to the State Department if necessary. Someone who might be able to tap into security organisations swapping info that impacted on Zimbabwe and Mozambique. Nothing illegal, of course, said Fred.'

'Really?' Paul said quizzically.

'Well, he didn't quite put it like that, but he talked about the Zimbabwe Central Intelligence Organisation, the CIO. Seems Sir Reggie has links into all these sources in the area. His main point was that Sir Reggie wants to keep on side with US policy makers, Mrs Thatcher's people and others who might influence regional activities. It was all a bit too high-politics for me, Paul, but I got his drift. So I made some enquiries amongst the other ex-pats living here and found Brad Trevelyan. He was happy to do some research for me.'

'What's his provenance?'

'As he said, ex-Langley. He was a Major-equivalent in rank. What he didn't say was that he screwed up in Afghanistan during the CIA's Operation Cyclone. Training the Mujahideen to combat the Soviets. Not sure it was his screw up to be frank. But you know the Yanks. They love to blame someone and they love to fire people.'

'What happened?'

'Brad saw things amongst the Mujahideen hierarchy and logistical support back in Pakistan that he thought were ominous. Ominous for the future. His personal belief was that the Mujahideen were quite capable of becoming a force in their own right, and would seize on the vacuum created by any Soviet withdrawal to build terror cells inside Afghanistan and link them to fundamental root support in Pakistan. His reports back to Langley were not appreciated, apparently. His voice was too dissident. And look at the place now. The Russians can't get out quick enough and all sorts of groups are swarming in to take their place, mainly funded by the State Department through the good offices of capitalist politicos like bloody Charlie Wilson, and others.'

'Did he do field work in Afghanistan?'

'He did; and that's the other reason why he fucked up. He killed a local Mujahideen leader in a bar fight in Kabul and had to be got out immediately.'

'Sounds like my kind of person,' Paul said and brightened. Trevelyan was going to be an asset after all, just as he'd thought. 'Was it justified?'

'Brad tells me it was. The Afghani didn't like Brad poking around with his contacts into Pakistan, the Yemen and Saudi Arabia. Christ knows how the Afghans found out what Brad was doing, but this particular Mujahideen leader did. Brad's theory was that exiled Islamic cells in these countries were going to be the next big threat. The man obviously had something to protect and hide and wanted Brad, with his information and theories, out of the way. He succeeded, as it happened, but got himself killed in the process.'

'How did he kill the man?'

'Cut his throat in a knife fight. Brad's a close combat specialist. He may look like a hippy dropout but he's far from that,' Dalloway paused and then went on. 'So he cut the man's throat and had to cut his official links with the CIA and came east into Nepal. But he's connected, Paul, I don't know how, but he is. And I need him to get up-to-date information about what's going on inside the commercial offices of the

Department of State, and to help build the business case for MozLon.'

'I agree, Danny. It sounds like you do need him.'

Paul had all the information he required, and at that moment the door to the room opened and Trevelyan and Omparsad entered.

'Got here early then, Paul? Everything OK?' the American offered with just a hint of suspicion in his tone and with a quizzical twist to his mouth.

'I did, Brad. There were some things I needed to get clear with Danny before we went any further. But that's all done now and everything is very well, thank you.' Paul looked to Omparsad. 'Did you get the information, Om?'

'I did, saheb. They are close.'

'Any luck with the goods, Brad?' Paul asked.

'I'll have them by early evening.'

Dalloway chipped in. 'All very mysterious, Paul.'

'It's best you don't know the detail of all this, Danny. There's black work to be done and you know nothing about it. You're in hospital, after all.' Paul turned to the Gurkha. 'Are we meeting as planned later, Om?'

'We are, saheb. Bhimbahadur says we can have the back room of the Tom & Jerry. He will make it secure and he will feed us.'

'Good.' Paul made a decision. 'Brad, we'll meet back at Bhimbahadur's bar by eighteen hundred hours. OK? I have to take Rup off again. I need to visit somewhere and then get back up to the guesthouse for some clothes.'

71

'Ok, Major, if that's what you gotta do. And eighteen hundred hours will be just fine.'

'One final thing, Om,' Paul stood and moved towards the door, 'we need to get into Bhimy's by a back entrance. And I need two of your boy's to be in the bar itself, just having a drink and keeping surveillance.' Paul took some money out of his wallet. 'Give them this money. And give the rest to Bhimy to cover all his costs.' Paul spoke to Dalloway. 'Rest easy, Danny. I'll see you again tomorrow.'

Paul left them. There was one piece of his plan he needed to recce further before the meeting tonight. Rup would take him to the Pashupatinath Temple on the banks of the Bagmati River and explain to him what happened there.

He would tell Paul all about how the dead must appease the Hindu gods.

7

THE STRIKE BACK

THEY CONFIRMED THE plan in the back room of Bhimbahadur's bar. They prepared and rehearsed all the contingencies. Omparsad brought the crucial information of where the Hungarians were living. Paul was happy. It was a bit rushed, but quite often in his experience the simplest plans, the most hastily put-together and straightforward in execution, worked the best. Anyway, they had no other options. The strike back was needed and needed immediately. It was now two-thirty the next morning, his third day in Kathmandu, and he wanted it to be his third-to-last.

One of things he had done in the afternoon after leaving the others was to visit a travel agent and confirm his return flight for the tenth. Whatever happened he was going to be on that day's flight to Bangkok. Then Rup had taken him to the Pashupatinath Temple and walked him through the areas where non-Hindus can go, and explained how it all worked. What he had found out was enough for Paul to complete the plan. He had done his time and space estimate and even in the best case he didn't think they could complete everything until the ninth, the day after tomorrow. So he was leaving on the tenth of

December. He just hoped the Hungarians were where they should be.

Gopal suddenly appeared out of the darkness of the alleyways and spoke to Omparsad. Paul could not make out his features; the camouflage cream had done its job. Paul had insisted on it; and on them all wearing dark, drab clothing and black woollen hats. Omparsad turned to him and whispered in his ear. 'We are close, saheb. The place is no more than two hundred metres from here.'

Paul crouched down, checked to see that Trevelyan was tucked into the side of the building and ushered the four of them backwards a few paces so that they slipped into a narrow side alley and huddled together in the shadow. 'Are the others in place?' Paul whispered to Gopal.

'They are, saheb. All is set.'

Paul looked up at the night sky. There was a half moon and it bathed the wall opposite them in its eerie light. He studied the silhouettes and crazy roof-outlines of the maze of buildings and listened to the sounds of the morning, but there was nothing to hear. It was the perfect time to be about this kind of business. They were in the heart of Kathmandu's Old Quarter, close by Durbar Square, where they had sat and talked yesterday; and it felt to Paul that the ancient place was granting him silence so they would not be interrupted in their task.

The square and the complex of palaces, courtyards and temples had been built many centuries ago by the ancient kings of Nepal. Now they housed, in amongst the ramble of buildings, the Hungarians. It was as if the old city wanted rid of these alien elements and was granting Paul and the others the silence, lack of disturbance and the half-moon light to do it. The Hungarians had rented a small apartment close by the Hanuman Dhoka, the Hanuman Gate, in this most ancient part of the city. Omparsad's scouts had located the building earlier yesterday by following one of the Hungarians. The surveillance ring had been in place ever since.

'Do we know that the *dushman* are inside?'

'The last man was seen going inside at zero zero-thirty hours, saheb,' replied Gopal. 'I have just checked with Kindraman, who is there, and he and the boys say three men are inside and no one has left since that time.' Half-past midnight, Paul thought, only two hours ago. He needed to give the enemy a bit more time.

During the earlier planning session in the Tom & Jerry back room, Omparsad had agreed to muster the additional Gurkhas required for the surveillance and support work. Paul had given Gopal and Kindraman the task of strengthening the surveillance net around the Hungarians, using some of these men. How they'd done it, Paul had no idea. But if Gopal said the enemy were in their place then they would be.

'OK, Gopal, good. Get back to them. Kindraman has the cart?' Paul had outlined his plan and they had all agreed a solid cart was needed; a hand-pulled cart, and Kindraman had been given the task of getting one and getting it to the right place and briefing the men he needed.

'Yes, saheb, and it will do the job. Kindraman has it hidden close by.'

'And you and he have told the others where you are to take it?'

'Yes, saheb. The plan will work. *Phikar na garnos,* saheb.' Do not worry. Paul *was* worried. Just a touch. There was no room for error here. Timing, as always, was everything, and so was logistics. But these were Gurkha soldiers, he reassured himself, they would give up their lives rather than let down their saheb or their comrades.

'Good. Remember, Gopal, no one, *no one* gets out of the building except us and no one gets in.' Paul was speaking lowly but the urgency in his voice was unmistakeable. 'Tell Kindraman to meet me at the entrance to the courtyard, as we planned.' The camouflaged Gurkha nodded his head and slipped away. Paul turned to Trevelyan and Omparsad. 'We need to give the Hungarians another thirty minutes. For all I know those bastard Slavs could be sitting up drinking bloody brandy or rum until daylight.'

'Might be to our advantage if they are, my friend,' which were the first words Trevelyan had spoken since they had left the Tom & Jerry; and he might be right, thought Paul.

In the shadow the three of them sat hunched down against the wall to wait. With their dark clothing and camouflage they were indistinguishable from the surrounding stone and brickwork. They were black shadows with blackened, dulled faces and clothed in black. Meanwhile the light of the moon played on the walls of the buildings opposite them.

Paul felt the lump of the Browning and its suppressor in the side pocket of his cargo trousers. The American had been true to his word and produced a worn but serviceable Browning 9mm pistol, one of Paul's favourite handguns. It was wrapped up in a dirty old rag, with the suppressor. Paul had immediately checked it for safety, emptied the bullets out of the magazine and tested its spring, and then stripped the pistol down to its remaining six pieces and held the barrel up to the dim light. It was clean and not pitted and there was a light sheen of gun oil. Then he had scrutinised each of the ten bullets, cleaned them with the rag and slotted them back in the magazine.

Trevelyan had chuckled. 'See you know that little baby well, Paul.'

'I do, Brad. It's saved my life on more than one occasion. And this one's clean. Well done and thanks.' Then he'd looked at the suppressor. He didn't like them. They were usually not a brilliant fit for the Browning, doubled the barrel length, almost doubled the weight of the weapon and reduced the muzzle velocity so much you needed to check the weapon had reloaded after firing. The only advantage was the ejected brass bullet cases would be easy to find; and what he planned would be close quarter work, so he was set up. The American had delivered. 'Are you armed, Brad?' he'd asked Trevelyan.

'Yes, I am, buddy,' Trevelyan had replied. 'If you think I'm going into any kind of a rough house without some type of personal weapon then you're crazier than I've been told. But it's the silent and deadly approach for me. I like it better.' And he'd produced a lethal looking skinning knife with a honed razor sharp edge. 'Also good for close quarter work, which I guess is what it's gonna be.'

Omparsad's words brought Paul back to the present. 'It is almost zero three hundred hours, saheb. Shall we move?'

Paul hadn't needed to ask the Gurkhas about their weapons. Earlier, he had witnessed Gopal and Kindraman sharpening their kukris with a small, well-worn whetstone. The blades would be lethal.

* * *

KINDRAMAN MET THEM and guided them into his hiding place in an old courtyard with a deep overhanging roof. There was another Gurkha there. Paul didn't know him but the two men nodded to each other.

Paul saw the big handcart with a pile of old blankets in the back. Four more Gurkhas were crouched, faces blackened, in its shadows. It would need at least four of them to pull it, with the remainder of the Gurkhas leading it from the front and shepherding it on from behind. It was fine, he thought, the numbers tallied; and there would be tasks for the others as well. The group moved back out from the courtyard and Paul saw Gopal. He must be across the street from the Hungarians' house. Kindraman's next words confirmed it.

'That is the *dushman* house, saheb,' he said, pointing to the ramshackle building that had been confirmed as the Hungarians' base. The doorway and eaves were picked out in the moonlight. Paul could see two windows facing onto the street and both were curtained. Kindraman then indicated where five other Gurkhas were posted. In this small square there were four narrow street approaches. Gopal and Kindraman had placed a man at each point of access and egress. It was a secluded spot, which was probably one of the reasons the Hungarians chose it. Now it was partially bathed in moonlight but it was secluded. Paul listened for the heartbeat of the Old Quarter but the place was still silent. The city was sleeping peacefully.

'They have their orders, Kindraman, yes? And they all know what to do?'

'*Je*, saheb, they do. The kukris have been sharpened and the boys will kill the *badmash* if they have to. No problem.' And with this Kindraman smiled a wide smile so that the brightness of his teeth broke the gloom, and he pulled out his kukri and ran his thumb gently down the edge of its wicked, curved blade, to make his point. A small blob of his blood formed on the blade. He wiped it off and re-sheathed the weapon. 'Leave some enemy for us, saheb, if you can.' And Paul knew the Gurkha was deadly serious. The Hungarians had attacked one of their sahebs and in so doing had committed a death-sin. But Paul had to protect these good men. They would kill mercilessly in the right cause, but they had to live here.

'Let's go,' Paul said to Trevelyan and Omparsad. He moved across towards Gopal. Omparsad had drawn his kukri and the cold steel glinted momentarily in the moonlight. Trevelyan had a small clump of blackened tools in one hand. His task was to jemmy any locks or catches on the doorway of the Hungarians' apartment.

During the planning the American had said he could do it and had the tools to do so. "Part of the black trade of Langley, Paul", he had said. Paul sniffed the air as they moved. It was a habit. He wanted to taste the atmosphere and let it work its effect upon him. The early morning air was frostily cold, clean and nipped him in his lungs. He could feel the adrenaline flowing gently and under control through his system. He was charged up. His senses were sharp, as they always were when danger was close. In the space of less than forty-eight hours he had gone from would-be tourist to intended-assassin in Kathmandu, but it didn't trouble his mind at all. It was three o'clock in the morning. It was the dead hour, the time of the day-night cycle when a person's resistance was absolutely at its lowest. It was the killing-time and he had killing to do.

Gopal joined them and then the four of them were at the doorway, two either side, crouched down, bodies pressed back into the darkness of the walls. Trevelyan moved in front of the door and kneeled down. Paul tapped his trouser pocket to feel the Browning again. His heart rate was quickening. Come on, Brad, he said to himself, get us in without us having to break the bloody thing down. Then the door creaked open and Trevelyan held its edge and turned to him and nodded. This was it. The American held the door open as if to usher Paul in. Thanks, he thought.

Speed or the cautious approach, Paul asked himself as he slipped into the dark entranceway of the house. They hadn't been able to get a detailed layout of the actual place, but from what they could find out, it was most likely the entrance led directly into stairs. They'd been told the living accommodations of these small apartments were almost always upstairs, possibly even two floors of it. And this was the same, he realised with small relief, as he edged into the gloom saw nothing but dirty, empty floor areas and then found the stairs leading upwards. There was a shaft of moonlight creeping down the stairs but there was more lighting, low room lighting, Paul saw, reflecting down into the stairway.

Paul motioned to Omparsad and Trevelyan to keep the spacing they'd agreed: close but not so close that any of them couldn't swing an arm or make a move. Gopal would stay by the door and guard it. He would be the reserve if needed. But Paul's plan was three on three. Surprise action, God willing, to take two out and leave the one he wanted to talk to, Mr Tamas Benko. Dalloway had described the Hungarians and Paul was certain he would recognise the man. He would recognise Virag Karas as well.

He got to the top of the stairs and looked quickly around to get the layout of what he now saw was the communal living space. He had been right, there were two hurricane lamps burning low in the far corners, which threw a dull light over the furniture in the centre of the room. Omparsad was behind him, with Trevelyan just at the top of the stairs. Across the room Paul counted three doors, all closed, one to his left and two dead ahead. He turned his head quickly from side-to-side and saw a galley area tucked back and to his left and a narrow corridor leading away to his right. Paul's instincts told him something was wrong because one of the old sofas in front of him had a heap of rumpled bedding on it. Shit, there's a fourth man. There has to be.

And there was, and Paul's plan momentarily faltered as a tall, thin-looking man wearing raggedy cotton pyjama trousers and a dirty cut-off T-shirt staggered into the living

81

area. There had been no flush of water. Damn! The man was dark-haired, Caucasian, and was rubbing his hands through his long greasy hair. At least it's not a woman, Paul thought. That would have made things very difficult. The man looked up and his mouth started to work. Paul instinctively stepped towards him but Omparsad was faster.

Like a mongoose striking a cobra the Gurkha leapt into the room and his kukri slashed downwards. It was a massive blow. It had all the force of his strong right arm and upper torso behind it, and was ripped downwards with the acceleration of his swinging shoulder motion. The blade cut through the man's left collarbone like butter and cleaved deeply into his chest and heart. It was a killing stroke and the man's breathing gurgled and frothed and blood formed in his open gasping mouth as he staggered and clutched at his wound, trying to speak or cry out. Omparsad was not finished. He wrenched the blade free and swung it again through the man's neck and the half-severed head dropped grotesquely as the body fell forwards.

Paul stepped around the staggering, lurching body. He went to stop it hitting the floor but Omparsad grabbed the man's T-shirt and lowered the body down. Blood was already pooling on the filthy throwdown rug from the appalling wounds. The man's eyes were glazed. He's as good as dead, Paul thought, but they'd made too much noise and he could hear some shuffling activity inside the furthest door to his right. Surprise was just about lost and speed and shock action was all they had left.

'Om,' Paul said quietly, 'take that small door on the left. If it's the main man then keep him alive, if you can.' The Gurkha was wiping his kukri blade on the dead man's clothing and nodded his head and moved behind Paul.

'I'll take the room to the right,' said Trevelyan. The American had come alongside him at the top of the stairs. Paul looked at him quickly. He appeared calm and unfazed and was already moving past the dead, bloody body on the floor with his skinning knife in his right hand.

'Thanks, Brad,' Paul said. The American grunted and stopped. The door in front of him opened and a medium-height, fat-bellied, half-naked man stood in the doorway yawning, and then froze. His expression of amazement was almost comical. Almost. 'It's not Benko, Brad,' Paul said, 'it's Karas, so take him. OK?' The American was already moving and before Karas could unfreeze his mind and cry out Trevelyan was in front of him. In a blur of movement Paul saw the American's arm come up into the big man's chest as the knife blade tore through the fat layers and under the ribs. And almost in the same movement Trevelyan stepped back from the lurching man whose arms were windmilling and punching and grasping to get hold of his assailant and slashed his knife blade across the man's throat and then kicked him in his bloody chest so that he fell heavily back into the room. The American leapt on him.

Paul was conscious in the periphery of his vision that Omparsad was at his door. He nodded once as if to signal to the Gurkha and then smashed his foot into the door in front of him, the one in the left corner, which looked like the largest, and if he guessed correctly, the leader's room. He felt it give instantly and followed it up with a massive shoulder charge that tore the flimsy wood off its hinges and left it hanging crookedly inwards. He had the Browning in his right hand but didn't intend to use it. Not just yet. He needed Benko and he needed some information. And then there was a man, there in front of him, standing back just inside the room. A tallish man, wearing some kind of shorts and a vest, but built like a racing greyhound, all muscle and sinew.

It was Benko. The Hungarian didn't speak but his eyes glinted in the low light. They looked jaundiced and evil. He's a man used to trouble, Paul thought, as Benko stood for a split-second, poised and on the verge of lunging forward. His eyes never left Paul's. He had a huge hunting knife in one hand and Paul's mind registered that it was probably the knife the Hungarian had used to maim and blind Dalloway. One thing was certain. Paul knew he couldn't get into a brawl with the man. He knew the type. Benko was without doubt a street fighter with the mentality and physical presence of one. He wasn't big and muscled but he was a gangster, and in Paul's experience gangsters could fight and fight dirty, and this man looked the part: shaven-headed and fight-scarred. He needed to be brought down as quickly as possible.

Paul stepped inside Benko's lurching knife stroke and brought the butt of the Browning down on the man's wrist with all his strength. He heard the wrist bone snap and saw the pain and shock register in the man's eyes and he smiled to himself as the knife clattered on the floor. Then he head-butted the Hungarian. Paul put all his upper body weight and forward momentum into the move. There was no point in doing it half-heartedly. He had learned this the hard way in the past, and ended up with a serious bout of concussion and a massive bruise on his forehead. "The frontal bone of the skull is hard", the doctor back at Hereford told them all, "and the enemy's nose doesn't stand a chance provided you have the courage of your convictions and use your head like a sledgehammer". And the man had been right. And was again now. Benko's nose burst back against his face and the man gasped out loud in even more shock and pain, his fighters' posture completely broken by the speed and ferocity of Paul's actions. He was staggering back into the room; but Paul was relentless now, his blood fury was up.

'And you thought you could hurt my friend, did you, you Hungarian bastard.' Paul half-turned to his left and with his right foot, trod downwards and sideways into the man's right kneecap. The hard-edged trekking boots, Paul's physical strength and the velocity of the move broke the Hungarian's kneecap. The anger he felt helped, too. He wanted to finish up what he had to do and get out of the place.

Benko was whimpering on the floor. 'So much for Slavic machismo, eh, Paul.' Paul turned to the sound of Trevelyan's voice. 'It seems that all these bastards are good for after all is playing cards, drinking shots and abusing their lovely women. Oh, and threatening those who want to do honest work. Piece of Hungarian shit.' The American was lounging against the doorway a sardonic smile on his face. Paul saw no sign of his knife.

'Your man, dead, Brad?'

'He is, my friend, very dead. So is Omparsad's. No contest there, buddy. The kukri wins over bare hands every time.' Paul felt his body start to relax. The adrenaline rush had peaked. The American continued. 'We've checked the rest of the place and it's clear. There's nothing up above either.'

'Good, and thanks.' Paul turned back to the Hungarian and spoke to Trevelyan as he looked at the man. 'Help me drag this scumbag out into the main room. He'll scream like a nancy girl but ignore him.' Then Paul seemed to have an idea. 'Wait a second.' He stepped around the Hungarian and into the room. 'This'll do,' he said as he found what he was looking for. 'Watch him, Brad,' and Paul stuffed an old vest into Benko's mouth. The man started to resist but Trevelyan trod down on his wrist and the man's body lurched forwards in agony. Paul flat-palmed the man's smashed nose and the Hungarian's eyes almost crossed with the pain. 'Stay still, you bastard,' Paul said, 'there's nothing but more pain for you. So wait for it and act like a man.' They dragged Benko out into the living area and dropped him. Paul looked for Omparsad. The Gurkha had brought the other three bodies together and laid them side-by-side at the top of the stairs. They were all on rugs. Good, thought Paul. 'Keep an eye on this one, Brad. Kill him if you need to, but please ask me first.'

'Roger that, boss man.'

Paul put the Browning back into his trousers' pocket and looked at his watch. It was almost four o'clock. He breathed deeply and felt the calm come back into his thoughts after the mad rush of violent action. 'Now for the final act,' he said to the others. 'Om, get Gopal and Kindraman and some of the boys up here. We need to get these three bodies into the cart. Use bedding to wrap them in, soak up any blood on the floors.' He turned back to Benko. 'Get him into a sitting position, Brad, back against the wall, where he should have been years ago. This pathetic human and I have some talking to do.'

8

BURN IN HELL

THE GURKHAS CAME back up the stairs, led by Omparsad, and immediately started gathering bedding and sheets and mummifying the dead Hungarians. It took them seconds. There was teamwork and fast efficiency in everything they did. The first of the bodies was carried down the stairs.

Paul felt a sudden wash of fatigue. It wasn't surprising. He'd hardly slept since he left London. He found a chair and pulled it over in front of Benko where Trevelyan had propped the broken Hungarian against the wall. The man's manner signalled pain and Paul realised he was choking since he could hardly breath through his smashed nose. Paul pulled the vest out of the man's mouth, picked up a cushion from one of the old sofas and put it on the chair and sat down. The American was smoking one his cheroots and looking totally relaxed. I *really* like this man's style, Paul thought once again. He and I could definitely work together again in the future.

'Danny Dalloway's a lucky man to have you on his side,' he said to Trevelyan.

'I'd say he is, and it's not me we're talking about here. It's having good buddies like you who'll come all the way over from London to deal with trash like this one here,' and the

American blew a funnel of black smoke over the watching Hungarian.

'What is it you are talking about?' Paul turned towards Benko as the man spoke the words in a nasal, rasping tone, choked with his pain. He'd almost forgotten the Hungarian had a voice. And Dalloway had been right, the man spoke English. He looked at the Hungarian and registered the feral hatred in the man's eyes. But there was something else there, too. Surprise? Confusion? Either side of the man's smashed nose his yellowed eyes were moving constantly between Paul and Trevelyan. Paul didn't know and didn't care what he was thinking or how confused he might be.

'Why have you come here, to this peaceful Kingdom with your plans to break apart other people's hard work and try to take what is not yours?' Benko looked at him and his eyes narrowed. 'Answer me.' Paul forced his will on the man. His words had an unavoidable edge to them. Yet the Hungarian tried to evade the meaning.

'Who are you all disguised like soldiers? And why do you beat me and kill my innocent friends?' Benko's English was good but heavily accented. Trevelyan snorted and puffed on his cheroot feverishly. The Gurkhas were quietly moving the bodies out.

'Because you made the mistake of threatening my friend's business activities and then you made an even bigger mistake by kidnapping him and hurting him so badly that he is now certain to lose half his sight.' Paul paused. 'Do you understand what I'm saying, Mr Tamas Benko from the sewers of Budapest?'

'What do you know about Budapest,' the Hungarian said, and spat blood and froth at Paul's feet.

'About as much as you know about Kathmandu, and about me,' and Paul got up and walked into Benko's bedroom, picked up the Hungarian's knife from the floor and stood in front of the man. He pushed the chair away. Now he could see deep fear in the yellow eyes. 'Is this the knife you used on Major Dalloway?' Paul asked. 'Is it?' The room had gone quiet. Trevelyan was rigid. Paul glanced to his side. Omparsad was watching impassively from across the room, where the Gurkhas paused in lifting the last of the dead bodies down the stairs. 'I'll ask you again, Benko. Is it?'

'Yes...' The man's voice was a failed broken croak and his face grimaced in anticipation.

Paul held the knife out to Trevelyan, gesturing for him to take it. 'Hell, Paul,' the American said, 'ain't you gonna use it to finish off this Slav toad? It's less than he deserves, after all.'

'No. I'm not.'

Omparsad stepped towards Paul and the momentary spell was broken. Paul looked at the Gurkha as he spoke. 'We must go, saheb. Let me kill this evil person.'

'We must, Om. But I have one more thing to find out. This man knows the answer. It is what you all need to hear.' Omparsad nodded and stepped back towards the stairs signalling to the Gurkhas to get on with carrying out the last body. Paul looked towards them and saw Gopal was there, also, standing and watching. 'You can go, Gopal, if you want.'

'I will stay, saheb.'

Paul nodded. He understood why the Gurkha wanted to be present for the final act. They had no concerns about violent killing as an act of retribution. But they had an honour code and they needed to see its requirements had been exacted. He turned his gaze back to the Hungarian. 'There were four of you, yes?'

'Yes.'

'Are there any more of your filthy brothers here or coming in from Budapest?'

'No. We were only four. We fled from Hungary. There are more back in Budapest but they wait for my messages. I am to tell them that it is good to come, that we have business here.'

'And if you do not send the messages?'

'Then they do not come. Simple. This is bizniz. We will go to another place where already there are more cousins, like me.' The expression on Benko's face told Paul that as he said it, the man realised what a stupid thing he had just admitted. Paul feigned to ignore its meaning.

'And those Manangis you used when you beat my friend?'

'They are not a part of us. They do not know what it is we do.'

Paul turned to Omparsad and Gopal. 'You can deal with the Manangis?' he asked. They both nodded. 'I thought so.' Paul stood and took the Browning out of his pocket and pulled the suppressor out of another. He fitted it quickly and then cocked the weapon and flicked off the safety catch.

'So the weapon wasn't even cocked?' said Trevelyan and chuckled.

Paul didn't bother to answer. This was his dark side at work. It was his job and it was what he had been trained for and he was good at it. But it was one of the reasons why Christina had left him. She just could not accept the dichotomies that worked inside him. But he felt no remorse, no worry that he might be shredding some of the substance of his soul. It was justice; but he wasn't going to lord over it. He spoke to Benko for the last time.

'You should never have come here and you should never have threatened or beaten my friend. And you can take this last thought with you. You will never see Budapest again because you will burn in hell.'

Benko leaned forwards as if in a final panic at the meaning of these words. Paul picked up the cushion from the chair put it behind Benko's head and pushed him back against the wall. He held the man there with his left hand and shot Benko between his eyes. It took seconds. The weapon re-cocked, which was a plus for him, and Paul fired a second shot just next to the first. To make sure. Paul never believed in not making sure. The Hungarian slumped sideways. The cordite tinged the foetid air of the room.

'Now that's what I call a proper job done,' said Trevelyan laconically and moved towards the body. 'Boy, that sure is an ugly face, now. Guess we'd better clean up some of this mess, boys.' The cushion behind the man's head was smeared with cranial bone, brain tissue and blood. Paul stood back. Omparsad called across to Gopal and the two Gurkhas picked up Benko's body and started binding it in blankets.

Paul unloaded the Browning and picked up the two brass cartridge cases. 'You need this back, Brad?'

'I do not, Major,' the American said with a chuckle. 'It can all go into the garbage disposal that we talked about, along with this knife.'

'Yes, it can,' Paul said and looked at the Gurkhas. 'We need to clean up, Om.' His mind was working coldly and thinking through the final moves they had all agreed. 'Take the cushion with all the other things. Check if the bullet heads went into the wall. Dig them out if they did. Then we have to remove every sign of these men; their passports, money, clothes, baggage, their food and drink, everything. They must disappear. The landlord can have his apartment back, but with no people. And it must be clean. Can we do this?'

'Of course, saheb,' said Omparsad. 'The boys have been briefed. But we must move quickly. They are waiting for us to leave so they can start. We have two hours only but they must be finished before then and be back secure at Bhimbahadur's.'

'They must also wash down the blood,' said Paul. 'Everything must go into the cart and be taken back to Bhimy's place. With these weapons. As we planned.'

'*Hunchha*, saheb. Give them to me and then let us leave so the boys can get on with it,' the Gurkha replied.

Paul suddenly felt empty. 'We will go to Pashupatinath tomorrow?'

'Yes, saheb, we will. I will be in charge and you can watch. You have done enough. Come, let us go.'

Trevelyan came up to Paul and touched his arm. Paul looked at the American and saw the stress and tiredness in his face and also the friendliness in his eyes. 'You've done real well, buddy, and I mean *real* well,' his voice was soft and earnest. 'That was some feat you accomplished there, and I mean it. Everything has turned out just copacetic.'

'I think I know what copacetic means, Brad, and so, yes, it has,' Paul replied, and felt some of the weight lift from his soul. 'And thank you for your assistance.' The American just smiled.

Paul followed the Gurkhas and Trevelyan down the stairs. He didn't look back.

* * *

PAUL FELT REFRESHED and the sunshine was welcome. He knew he looked rough - shagged out would be a more apt description - because he'd finally shaved that morning and had the chance to look at himself in the small mirror in his room at the Kathmandu Guest House. This was his fourth day in Kathmandu and he'd had no more than sixteen hours sleep. His bent nose and his close-cut fair hair were familiar. But his weather-blue eyes had peered back at him from inside deep, black smudged holes, and his face had looked tired and stressed. It was almost a face he hadn't recognised, a stranger's face.

As he'd scraped the beard-stubble off with his razor he'd reviewed how it had all happened and been surprised, if he was honest, at how things had worked out. Not bad considering it was all done on the hoof and from a standing start. But that's Gurkhas for you, Stanton, he admitted, they just do things right!

Now he was out in the sunshine with Brad and Rup in the Pashupatinath Temple looking over the *ghats* on the banks of the Bagmati River. As far as he could see all around him were the buildings and grounds of the main Temple and all the smaller places of pilgrimage and homage. The whole area was thronged with thousands of people and the colour and vibrancy of it all seemed like a minor miracle of transformation after the dark deeds of the days and nights before.

Dotted in amongst the smaller temples in their little alcoves, sat the *sadhus*, with their garishly painted faces and bodies and matted, filthy hair, their reeking rags wrapped sparsely around their emaciated frames. They sat in the lotus position in prayer and meditation, occasionally getting up to move around or wander down to the river to wash and squat. In front of their positions the constant stream of visitors had placed garlands of marigolds, fruit and flower petals as offerings for wisdom and blessing. They may offer a more lofty perspective on spiritual life, Paul thought, but having seen the relish with which these holy mystics exposed their private parts in the face of the young women who came to see them, he had a more cynical view of them. They were dirty old buggers! No question about it.

'I gotta hand it to you, Paul, it was a totally inspired part of the plan,' said Trevelyan.

'It was!' Paul couldn't help but take the applause.

'I'd never have thought of it, buddy, and it's working well, so it is.'

It *had* been inspired. 'But it was Rup's guided tour the other day that gave me the idea,' said Paul. The little taxi driver looked at him. The Nepali understood what they were saying but he didn't know *quite* how he had helped them. 'It's all to do with the coming *Poornima* Festival.'

'Yeh, I kinda guessed that we needed to have people around the place and a lotta activity goin' on.' The American's slight drawl had reappeared, and Paul chuckled at it. 'And that's this *Poornima* thing, I'm thinking. Am I right?'

'You are. But I'll let Rup tell it,' Paul said. He turned to the taxi driver. 'Rup, please explain to Mr Trevelyan what is so sacred about this place where we are standing. Tell him also about *Poornima*.'

Paul had learned over the past few days in the company of Rup that the man was blessed with unusual self-confidence and a pride in his night-school-attained ability in the English language. Whilst not a martial Gurkha, Rup was remarkable in so many ways, as Paul had discovered. Paul had quizzed the little man constantly, whilst searching in his mind and the city for a way to dispose of the evidence of what he knew had to be done. Rup had brought Paul to Pashupatinath, walked him around, and the two of them had watched what was going on and the final piece in Paul's plan had fallen into place.

'It is coming to be a full moon, saheb,' Rup began, 'and it is the month of *Kartik*. And at *Kartik-Poornima* all the Hindus from all over Nepal and sometimes from India, they come here to Pashupatinath.' Trevelyan lit a cheroot and fixed the Nepali with a quizzical eye. Paul looked down to the riverbank. He could see it all and it was going well, as Trevelyan had said. He tuned back into the Nepali's monologue as Rup continued. 'It is a holy place for Hindus and the people they must bathe in the sacred waters of the Bagmati River and many will also come to do the ceremonial marriage of the *Tulsi* to *Vishnu* or *Krishna*.'

The American chipped in. 'Well I sure do applaud you on your English speaking, Rup, but I got two things to say right away. One I don't understand any of this marriage malarkey to gods, and two,' he looked at the river below them and pointed with his cheroot, 'that may be sacred to you fellas, but to me it's chock full of human debris and matted weed. You wouldn't get me bathing in that if my life depended upon it. Vishnu-only-knows what diseases are lurking in them waters.' Paul laughed out loud.

Rup looked a little nonplussed, so Paul came to his rescue and brought all their attentions back to the reason why they were standing in that particular spot. 'Forget about marriages and all that, Brad, we are looking at the *Bhasmeshvar Ghat*. The part of the Pashupatinath Temple where Hindus cremate their dead, and as you can see it is a very popular spot and there are a lot of cremations going on.'

'You can say that again, partner, and most of them seem to be ours,' at which Trevelyan laughed out loud at his own warped humour.

'Well, four of them are...' and Paul and the American laughed together at the irony and black humour and Rup smiled an inscrutable smile.

'As I said, buddy, totally inspired!'

'It was; but not without sacrifices on the part of Omparsad and the other Gurkhas. Look at them.' Paul pointed at the four burning *ghats* directly below where they stood. The concreted plinths were set no more than fifteen feet apart and there were at least twenty of them all told, and all in use. 'Looks like we have centre burning stage today,' he said, 'open air cremation on a grand scale with our Gurkhas as the family witnesses of the deceased.' Trevelyan laughed again.

'Oh boy. You sure have a funny way of saying things! Jeez but it feels good to laugh again.' And Paul had to agree. It did.

Each cremation site had a loin-clothed attendant who had built the framework of burning wood onto which the Gurkhas had laid the shrouded bodies of the four Hungarians. There were four Gurkhas at each *ghat*, the ones who had been involved in the execution of Paul's plan. They included Omparsad, who had taken on the responsibility of coordination for it all. Neither Gopal nor Kindraman were there, Paul noted, and he knew the reason why. As a sign of respect and cleanliness to the gods the Gurkhas had all shaved their heads, leaving only the tuft of the topknot. They looked suitably solemn. Once the ritual prayers and farewells had been said, the oil had been poured onto the wood and the fires lit. Paul and the other two had watched the complete performance. Now it was almost over and the *ghat* attendants were getting ready to shovel the burnt remains into the Bagmati River. They would smash up the bone fragments so the Holy River could wash them away more easily. It was, Paul thought, a fitting end for the bastards. Just a heap of washed away ash and bone bits.

'As you said it, Paul, burn in hell.'

Paul took a few seconds to register how well things had turned out. 'Yes, indeed. And that's one of the reasons why the bloody river's so full of rubbish,' Paul said. 'But at least we managed to get rid of all the other evidence as well.' Trevelyan nodded and puffed on his smoke. The hardware from the strike on the Hungarians had gone into the deepest and most remote part of the River on the edge of the city. The clothing and all their documentation were now ashes, about to be shovelled into the Bagmati along with the charred bone fragments. True to form the Gurkhas had recycled the other possessions cleared out of the Hungarians' apartment. It was a pity to waste it and Paul had agreed.

'Do you think Omparsad will ever forgive me for the fact he had to shave his head?'

'No, buddy, I doubt he ever will!'

9

HOME FOR CHRISTMAS

THE WOMAN WAS sitting in the chair next to Danny Dalloway's bed and she turned her head to the door as Paul opened it and stepped into the room. She was quick thinking.

'So you're Major Paul Stanton?' She was also very attractive, he thought, but not conventionally so.

'I am.' Paul paused. The woman stood up and faced him and was openly studying him. She was a touch above medium height, maybe five foot seven, possibly nudging eight, Paul guessed. Her hair was light brown, tending to blond, almost, and was thick and framed her oval-shaped face. Her eyes were the colour of mint chocolate, and sparkled as the filtered sunlight in the room caught the flecks of emerald green. She had a small, narrow-shaped nose, which matched her mouth and made her face look completely in balance. She spoke in a nondescript English accent. Her posture was slightly flirtatious, he thought, as she stood with her hands on her hips and her head cocked slightly, and as a small smile broke across her mouth and cheekbones. Or was he imagining it? 'And you must be Nikki Walker-Haig?' As Paul said the woman's name Dalloway's words came back to him and despite himself he felt gentle laughter bubbling inside. It must have showed on his face.

'Steady, Paul, steady,' chipped in Dalloway, pushing himself up on his pillows to watch this developing interplay. Paul felt himself under scrutiny and his smile broadened. He couldn't help it. A sense of devilment started to grow inside his brain. Nikki Double Scotch was the best thing he'd seen in a very long time.

'Hmm,' the woman pursed her lips and her eyes smiled playfully back at Paul. 'I'm guessing from that rather supercilious look on your face that Major Dalloway has told you what he rather disparagingly calls me.' The woman turned back towards the bed and flapped an arm at Dalloway and smiled.

Paul noticed several things all at once. Her hand was slim and her fingers well formed with clipped nails. It was her left hand and she was wearing only a small gold signet ring on her little finger. Why had he even looked? And she was slim with a great-looking body. Christ, Stanton, you've been working in the Ministry of Defence for too long.

'Well I happen to like whisky very much.'

'Bravo, Paul, bravo, absolutely fucking brilliant!' roared Dalloway. The woman frowned half-sternly at Dalloway's language and looked back at Paul. She put both hands back on her hips and studied him again. He felt himself responding. Even in faded jeans, walking boots and a locally made, waist-length soft woollen jacket over an open-necked well-washed cotton shirt, she looked great.

'Very much indeed, as it happens,' Paul said and the bubble of devilment he felt popped. He couldn't resist it. 'I especially like doubles.'

'Epic, Stanton, totally great!' Dalloway was struggling to keep his face straight against the strictures of his plaster, stitches and padding. Even Nikki Walker-Haig was nodding her head in amused appreciation. Dalloway was clapping.

'Well in that case, we might get on very well,' she said and held out her hand.

'I certainly hope so,' Paul said, and took her small hand in his and gently shook it. Her eyes held his and gave back small signals. He started to wish he wasn't leaving in three hours.

'True to form it looks like I'm leaving yet another party too early, just as the company starts to get interesting,' he said. Nikki Walker-Haig frowned questioningly.

'What he means, my darling Nikki, is that our mysterious, bent-nosed hero, here, who along with our intrepid Gurkhas and the quiet American has saved our bacon, is on the flight out to Bangkok this afternoon and isn't planning to come back any time soon.'

The woman looked at Paul. 'You're leaving this afternoon?' There was a trace of surprise in her tone, Paul read it there, and a small frown furrowed her brow.

'Unfortunately, yes, I am.' Suddenly Paul had a sense of a life-moment slipping away from him, and he had no idea how to try and grab the coat tails of this situation before its fabric slipped through his fingers. Bismarck's famous quote flashed through his mind. Dalloway rescued him.

'But you will come back, Paul?'

'I will?' Paul replied stupidly.

'Yes, yes, you will,' Nikki Walker-Haig said with evident relief. 'You must, surely.' Then she tried to find the follow on words. 'I mean, here you are, you came all the way out to Kathmandu when Danny asked you to. You somehow got rid of those evil Hungarians who were threatening to stop Danny's business before it had even got really started, so in a way...' she stumbled to a halt.

'So in a way, Paul, you're a part of our enterprise, even if it is as a visiting partner. How about that for a reason to come back,' said Dalloway triumphantly. 'And don't forget, my old mate, who dares wins, and all that SAS stuff!' And the man laughed.

Paul did, too. 'I'll do my best to come back, Danny. And I'll look forward to seeing you again, Nikki. I hope you'll still be here when I do. But if I can't make it then I'm sure we'll meet again someday. After all, your Company is going to be big business soon.' He moved over to the bed where Dalloway lay propped up on his pillows, conscious of her closeness. She smelled warm and fresh. He was glad he had shaved and put clean clothing on for the journey home. 'I'm off, Danny. And I'm really sorry you had to suffer like this. If we'd known we could have done something sooner, and maybe...'

'My fault, Paul. Totally my fault. I had no idea they would act so quickly. Just goes to show you can't trust a fucking Slav.'

'Danny!' the woman gently reproached him.

'She's a proper girl, this one, Paul, doesn't like my occasional profanities. Fails to see the necessary points of emphasis the good old F-word adds to our glorious language. Just as well you don't swear. Anyway, my old mate,' Dalloway continued as he shook Paul's hand, 'a million thanks. I know I'm going to be held up in here for a while, but Nikki is good, better than me at sorting out the business side. Bloody great in fact. Brad's a trump card and the boys, the good old Gurkhas, will hold it all together. We'll seal the deal with MozLon, I'm certain of it. We've still got two weeks to get the proposal into great shape and Nikki's a master at the wording.'

Dalloway held Paul's hand in his grip for a moment longer and his good eye blazed out of its horrendously damaged surrounds and fixed Paul with the intensity of his thoughts.

Paul cocked his head and said, 'You will.'

'You're damned right we will. I'm calling it GCL, Gurkha Connections Limited. We *are* going to be in business, Paul. Good business and we're going to make some money for our people here and we're going to help Sir Reggie Hanlon and his MozLon corporation make money, of course, but also do good for the people of Mozambique.'

'You will, Danny,' Paul repeated, 'I'm sure you will.' Paul turned to the woman. She must have read his face.

'I'll see you out, Paul. Let me at least say goodbye.' Dalloway raised his hand in farewell to Paul and winked with his good eye as Paul and Nikki Walker-Haig left the room.

She stopped him in the corridor outside, out of earshot, and looked into his eyes. 'I didn't know you were leaving today.' It was a flat statement but it didn't totally mask the emotion in her voice.

'I didn't know you existed outside of Danny's word description, until today,' Paul replied lamely.

'So that's the reason,' she replied enigmatically.

'What do you mean?'

'The reason why you're not staying.'

'Possibly.' Paul hesitated and then said, 'Actually, probably.' Paul knew he was playing a dangerous game here but his instincts told him it was the right thing to do and his instincts seldom failed him. 'But I wish I could stay.'

'So do I. Because I rather like you, Major Paul Stanton. I think you are a good man.'

'Thank you. But this time I have to return to London.'

'I know. But come back. Please.' And Nikki Walker-Haig reached up and put her arms around Paul's neck and pulled his face gently down towards hers. Paul felt a rush of emotion flood his system. The woman was overwhelming him. Her breath was warm and fresh and he stared into the kaleidoscope of her green-flecked eyes as she spoke. 'You have done a brilliant thing in coming here and helping us. Brad, the Gurkhas, Danny, poor, poor Danny, love you for what you did. Maybe that's a woman speaking, I don't know, but I wasn't here, and if I had been I would have been rooting for you all the way, Paul Stanton.' She stopped and Paul saw the high blush in her cheeks. 'Goodbye,' she said, 'for now,' and she pulled his face to hers and kissed him firmly and sweetly on the lips.

'Goodbye, Nikki.'

'At least you'll be home for Christmas,' she said. 'So think of us when you get back and then make a resolution in the New Year to come and see us sometime very soon after, please.'

'I will try my very best,' Paul said, and realised he meant it all. Two commitments. Spoken and agreed on. He released himself from her warm hands, turned and left. This woman had, in an instant, ignited his emotions.

But he had a plane to catch.

He had helped Danny Dalloway in his time of need and would be home for Christmas. Not only that, he'd be back in time to get up to the Scottish Borders to Melvilltown, to talk to the dead, as he always did on the 15th December, if he possibly could.

He smiled to himself at all the good thoughts that now filled his mind, and at the image he held there of the woman's face. Would he see her again? Certainly, he had to, and he'd already decided this. It would be in 1989, which wasn't too long to wait.

But Paul Stanton had no idea that it would only be seven months before he saw Nikki Walker-Haig again and that the events of 1989 would irrevocably change his life.

PART II - ENGLAND

THE GREAT TRAIN ROBBER

10

27TH APRIL 1979

27TH APRIL 1979.

Captain Paul Stanton knew the date and the day. It was a Friday and it meant there were only three more weeks of this jungle training to survive. It couldn't come soon enough.

Paul Stanton was twenty-six, fit as a flea and mentally tough, but he'd almost been brought to his knees by the rigours of the Brunei jungle. He'd come through the so-called Aptitude Phase, a month of intended physical destruction in the Brecon Beacons and was now six weeks into the Jungle Training, which was destruction of an entirely different kind. The jungle environment was corrosive. It rotted your clothes and equipment, your body and will. The training in survival skills, movement and tactics were unlike anything else in the British Army because the jungle was unique and unforgiving. Everything was done at a range of ten metres, often less, and there was no respite during daylight hours. Thank Christ it got dark early. Then all you had to contend with was the bible-black claustrophobia, tropical rains, swarms of mosquitoes and every crawling, biting, venomous, creature God had ever created. It was pure joy.

Physically Paul Stanton was a mess and the thought of another three weeks filled him with deep despair. But he'd do it. He'd told himself he would and so he would. But yes, he knew it was a Friday afternoon and he knew the date because he was ticking off the weeks in his mental calendar. It was helping him retain his sanity.

Up to his waist in filthy mangrove swamp, Paul and his patrol were navigating their way towards the river line, where, as soon as they hit it, they'd be lifted out by assault boats and taken back to their hutted camp at Tutong. They could hear the roar of the outboards, so they were close. He gritted his teeth, put aside thoughts of leeches worming their way through the bootlace holes in his jungle boots, and checked that he still had all his patrol with him. They were there close behind him, and struggling through the swamp. They looked as frightful and shagged out as he felt. Once back at Tutong they'd have thirty-six hours to repair their wasted bodies, sort out their kit and prepare themselves for the next week of training.

But first, get to the river line and the assault boats.

Paul had decided almost a year earlier that he wanted to try for SAS Selection. He'd been to the surreal warzone of Northern Ireland twice already with his battalion, the Scottish Infantry, and wanted to do more. His Commanding Officer had told him he had a brain and a talent for soldiering, that he had the time now to do something different before the prospect of the Staff College, and had supported the application.

This was SAS Selection, Paul had been reminded, the hardest Special Forces selection course in the world, six months of assessments designed to break most mortal men and reward those few who passed with that signal badge of honour of being a member of 22 Special Air Service Regiment, 22 SAS. Was he up to it? Paul had said yes and he wouldn't let the Regiment down. So he'd prepared himself for the best part of a year before Selection had started. Now, eleven weeks later here he was, having his blood sucked by leeches and being bitten to buggery by mosquitoes. Three more weeks of this hell and then still another fourteen weeks of Employment Training before he would be badged SAS.

Before he would become a Pilgrim.

Oh yes, he was up to it, and he'd pass the course, but one week at a time.

* * *

ON THAT SAME April Friday afternoon, on the other side of the world, over eleven thousand miles away in England, an horrific road traffic accident was claiming the lives of six people.

The accident was one of those million-to-one-chance events, which, as such events do, destroyed families. But it also revealed long hidden truths and unleashed unforeseen consequences. Improbably and ten years later, these consequences would impact dramatically in Paul Stanton's life.

So what happened?

* * *

A MARRIED COUPLE were driving back from a family visit in Cardiff to their home in Kew Green, London. They were on the M4 motorway and the husband was driving his latest model Porsche. He was forty-four years old and the beautiful wife at his side was twenty-eight. They were successful in the business in which they both worked, and were happily in love.

At the same time, a Mercedes was travelling westwards on the M4 carrying another husband and wife and their two young children. They were getting out of London for the weekend.

Suddenly the Mercedes swerved and hit the central crash barrier at the precise point where it had been bent downwards in some earlier collision. The car took off like a skier on a jump ramp, turning upside down as it hurtled through the air across the motorway's central reservation. In the blink of an eye, the Mercedes smashed into the front of the oncoming Porsche like a thunderbolt.

The combination of forces that acted on the two vehicles in those horrific moments of the crash was lethal. Everyone was killed. Instantly. Although it was an appalling and improbable accident, it had a special significance, because the identities of the people involved aroused national interest.

The woman in the Mercedes was the daughter of Raymond Bessone, known widely and famously as Teasy Weasy. Teasy Weasy Raymond was the celebrated Mayfair hairdresser and part owner of two Grand National winners. Because he was so well known, it seemed, the public outpouring of sympathy for the death of his daughter and her family was considerable.

The couple in the Porsche were Mr Brian Carlton and his wife Sian, to all who knew them, just a normal working couple with no children. Of course Sian's family in her hometown in Wales was devastated by the loss of their daughter, and they and her friends properly mourned her. But the curious thing was that no one, other than a few work colleagues and friends in their local pub in Kew, seemed to know very much about her husband, Brian Carlton. Where was his family? Who actually was he?

It took the authorities just over nine weeks to discover that Brian Carlton was really someone else. On the 3rd July 1979 it was revealed to the press that Brian Carlton was one of the Great Train Robbers.

Brian Carlton was in fact Brian Field, the gang member who had been pivotal in setting up and helping execute the Great Train Robbery. It was Brian Field who was the crucial link between the Royal Mail informant, the Ulsterman, and the gang leader Bruce Reynolds. Field also knew the other key gang members, Gordon Goody, Buster Edwards and Charlie Wilson. It was Field who arranged for the gang's escape with the loot, who purchased the hideout at Leatherslade Farm, and who was entrusted with its clean up, which he botched. Brian Field had been arrested and gone to prison and on his release in 1967 he had quickly changed his name to Brian Carlton, thus ensuring Brian Field completely disappeared.

Which was a wise thing to do at that time, because all the other Great Train Robbers who had been imprisoned - and not escaped - had also served their sentences and been released from jail, and they might have wanted to know what Field had done with the money he'd been asked to pass on to certain people. In the division of the banknotes after the heist, Field had been given his one-seventeenth of the haul and been entrusted to pay shares to others outside the gang who had played a part in the Robbery. But Field had kept their payouts for himself. The money in question had never reached its intended recipients, but neither had it ever been recovered. So where was it? What had Brian Field done with it?

It seemed no one, apart from Field-Carlton, knew. And now, with his death, no one would.

But was this the case?

* * *

STRUGGLING TO GET through the mangrove swamp in the Brunei jungle, separated from the real world, Paul Stanton could have no knowledge of the accident in which Brian Carlton-Field and his wife were killed.

And even though he would be back in the UK when the revelations of Carlton's true identity were made public, Paul would be far too busy earning his SAS beret to be interested in the media reportage. It was the summer of 1979, and with the end of Selection in sight, the world of action and adventure was just about to open up before him.

The problem was, that at that time, a young woman would begin to learn the truth about the man, Brian Carlton, with whom she had been working before his death. And ten years later, exactly ten years later on 3rd July 1989, this woman would be in trouble, and she would turn to Paul Stanton to help her in her time of need.

11

3RD JULY 1989

THE BUSINESS OF the Ministry of Defence in 1989 had kept Major Paul Stanton chained to his desk in Whitehall. As the decade moved towards its close, the status quo at home and abroad was changing dramatically. His work was fascinating, but frantic and always high priority, and he worked all the hours in the day, as did his fellow career officers. No one rested. Everyone around him was caught up in the crushing mill that was Whitehall.

The introduction of Mrs Thatcher's Poll Tax in Scotland had resulted in the unions' call for mass non-payment, and the Government's planned introduction of the community charge in England and Wales next year was widely expected to result in significant civil unrest. Although Paul's desk in Whitehall was not directly responsible for home socio-military affairs, they all kept a weather eye on such important issues because any threat to the PM's hold on power - in her cabinet and in the country - would have direct impact on the UK's military. There was a feeling in certain quarters that the end of the Thatcherite era was not far away. Paul listened intently to all the talk and tried to pick out the facts.

Northern Ireland was still as brutal and unrelenting as ever in its killing of security forces and its draw on manpower and resources, but the Government supported the effort, and long may it continue to do so the warriors in Whitehall said. Paul knew all about this: he'd had four tours in Ulster already and fully expected to serve there again. He'd almost been killed as a result of the Long War and he hated with passion those who claimed to practise the Catholic faith, whilst marching under the banner of the Republican Cause and casually murdering and maiming British soldiers and UK citizens with inhuman impunity. The widely held view was that the Provisional IRA would be emboldened by any weakening of Mrs Thatcher's position and her determination to force through the Anglo-Irish Agreement. Their attacks would inevitably have to take another form to capitalise on this perceived opportunity.

In Paul's experience, the IRA always adapted their tactics and advanced their technological edge. They would continue to kill and destroy. That was a given, the bastards; but in truth, as Paul and the others who watched knew, the IRA was in its final phase of the War. Politics was becoming more and more the vital trading goods of a beaten body. More blood would be spilled, but it would be a trickle not a river.

Then there was what was happening in Europe, in the East, which was where Paul's responsibility lay. Communism was unravelling. The Soviets had withdrawn finally from Kabul and their nine-year occupation-conflict in Afghanistan had ended in ignominious defeat. Well, Paul had mused at the time, The Great Bear joins the Mighty Lion of the British

Empire in leaving that tribal war zone in the foothills of the Hindu Kush with its tail between its legs. Except of course the Brits had lost three campaigns there. Didn't any nation's leaders ever learn from history? No, was the emphatic answer! But it was symptomatic in a way of the rapid decline in Soviet hegemony in Eastern Europe.

In Poland, the Solidarity Movement had won the country's first free elections since the late 1920s. And in May 1989, two months ago, the first crack in the Iron Curtain appeared as Hungary dismantled one hundred and fifty kilometres of the barbed wire fencing along its border with Austria and the exodus from East to West began. The mandarins in Whitehall believed it wouldn't be long before the Wall would come tumbling down.

It seemed to Paul that every one of these events in some way was woven into the story of his life in the past three years. First it had been the Wall in West Berlin, where he had ended the manhunt for those who had betrayed the security of his plans in Northern Ireland, resulting in the deaths of his men. Those had been dark and dangerous days. He had almost died at the hands of a deadly German criminal.

Then most recently it had been the Hungarians, mafia hoods to be precise, who had brought Paul to Kathmandu last December. He and his Gurkhas had killed the Hungarians, four of them, with the help of the quiet American, Brad Trevelyan. They'd had to. His old ex-Gurkha pal, Major Danny Dalloway, had to be avenged and his business interests protected from the greed of these brutal thugs. The Hungarians wanted a share of Danny's evolving business, and

117

to reinforce their claim had slashed out his left eye cutting his face from forehead to cheekbone.

It was unacceptable; so Paul had made a plan and the Hungarians had been killed, then burned in death and sent to Hell. It had been a swift, lethal operation and no one but those involved knew of it. With the exception of Nikki Walker-Haig, Dalloway's business assistant. She knew of it, and Paul had made a promise to her that he'd not kept, which was not his way. He'd met her just as he was leaving Kathmandu.

He remembered their words exactly; they had been ringing in his mind endlessly on and off for the last seven months. "So think of us when you get back and then make a resolution in the New Year to come and see us sometime very soon after, please," she had said. Their brief goodbye kiss had been firm and sweet. Her eyes were brown with hints of green when the light caught her face and her look had been serious. "I will try my very best," Paul had replied, and he'd really meant it because in the short time they were together this woman had stirred his heart.

But so far this year he'd been unable to return to Nepal; it had just not been possible and the failure to keep his promise had chastened him. He thought of what he'd said to her and he knew he should have tried harder to go. The fact was he'd been unable to break free from his work for long enough to travel, so he'd not seen Nikki Double Scotch, as Dalloway teasingly named her, since that time last December.

Until four days ago, that was, here in London. She had surprised and embarrassed him by telephoning unexpectedly whilst he was at work and saying: "You're not forgiven, Paul

Stanton, but I do understand you might have been busy. I'm in London for Danny's business meetings with MozLon next week. Can we meet?"

So they did. She had accepted the offer to come to his flat for a few days and use it as a place to stay and a base for her work. Then it all got complicated, and as a result Paul's failed word seemed irrelevant.

They became lovers.

* * *

PAUL LAY IN their bed in the summer sunlight of the early July morning. The 3rd July 1989. He felt a surge of affection for this wonderful woman and turned on his side to hug her tightly.

'You're not starting to get naughty again are you, Major Stanton?'

'Hmm, I might be,' Paul muttered, as he felt the soft curves of her bottom pushing firmly into his stomach and the nerve sensors in his brain sent out the appropriate messages, making his body stir. It was a sensuous, sexy feeling, a total sensation he'd never experienced the like of before. It made him feel protective yet it stimulated him at the same time. He folded his arm across her breasts and felt the stiffness of her nipples. Then he roved his hand downwards and stroked her thigh and her bottom pushed even more firmly into the cleft formed by his groin and stomach. He clasped her whole body to him tightly and languished in the texture and feel of her. She was voluptuously soft yet her body was firm and taught.

How could it be? It was an intoxicating physical experience and his soul sighed with contentment.

'Steady, lover boy,' she said. 'Release me from this strong-arm hold and let me be! Do something useful and get the morning paper. Remove your dodgy hands from my body and go about your duties!'

She turned her body towards him and looked at him with a mix of mockery and seriousness on her face and he saw the depths of her feelings in the mint-brown flecks of her eyes. He was falling suddenly and almost inexplicably in love with this woman and maybe, he thought, she was with him.

'I'm on my way, boss.' Paul stretched out on his back and looked through the open window where the listless curtains were drawn back to let in as much air as possible. But there was no movement. It was eight-thirty in the morning and already the sun was high in the London sky and the air was warm, and getting warmer. 'Monday morning,' he said. 'It feels weird not to be in the office.' Paul swung his legs over the edge of the bed and carefully rearranged the duvet so that Nikki was covered. She responded by throwing it off and lying naked and provocatively with her legs apart and her arms stretched out above her head in a most carefree and stimulating pose. 'You're very definitely bad for a career officer's career, Miss Double Scotch,' Paul chuckled.

'Come off it, Stanton. You're on leave, and you love it and me, admit it. And do you honestly have a career?'

'Well,' he said, 'I might, but don't bank on it.' Paul hadn't felt so happy for as long as he could remember. He sighed with contentment and went over to the open window.

'Be careful you don't frighten the natives, Paul.'

He laughed. 'This is Pimlico, Nik, 17 Lupus Street to be precise, just a ten-minute walk from that hub of fashionista London, Sloane Square, the heart of wild goings-on and absurd behaviour. Well it's where the SAS hang out for a start. It may appear to many to be a quiet residential area with an interesting architectural mix...'

'A what?' interrupted Nikki with a half-constrained snort of mock derision.

Paul turned to look at her and continued in a similar light-hearted way. 'As I was saying, Pimlico may appear to be quiet but it has housed in its history the likes of Aubrey Beardsley, Winston Churchill and Joseph Conrad, no less. Then there was Lawrence Olivier who lived in this very street four houses up. Nothing quiet or normal about any of that lot.'

'And now it houses Major Paul Stanton, MC, SAS. Is he, perchance, a quiet man?'

'Do not mock nor judge, you bad woman, Nicola. And yes I am quiet.'

'Hah, hah, Stanton. Not from what I've heard!'

'Do not believe everything you hear from the likes of that reprobate boss of yours in Kathmandu. If ever a man was a walking tactical nuclear fall-out zone, it's Danny Dalloway. Me,' he smiled beguilingly at her and flexed his chest and arm muscles in a simulated pose of a he-man, 'I'm a pussy-cat.'

'Bad, bad man, Stanton, you are definitely very naughty. Wash your mouth out with soap. I'll have no pussy-talk or the like from you.' Nikki sat up in the bed and her soft, small breasts with their hard-tipped nipples hung down a

121

fraction, tantalisingly, as if teasing his heightened senses. Her brown-blond hair was all over the place and he thought she looked absolutely beautiful. 'Stop gawping! Go and get the news and bring me coffee,' she said. Paul moved towards the bed. 'And stay away from me with that smug look on your battered face and stop throwing that sinewy, scarred body of yours at me. It has no effect. Go on, off with you!'

Paul laughed out loud and made to move from the bedroom towards the bathroom where his clothes were. 'You know why my face is battered, as you so delightfully put it?'

'Tell me, lover boy.'

'Too many boxing matches and too many head-butts in the cause of self-defence.'

'Well, more fool you, Stanton.'

'No, it's true. The doctor at Hereford always said that you must use your forehead like a sledgehammer, that it was one of the hardest bones in the body. So if you must head-butt an enemy then do it with ferocity and violence,' and Paul lurched forwards in a mock demonstration. Nikki grimaced. 'But it didn't mean that every now and then you wouldn't break your nose in the process,' and Paul laughed gently.

'So what happened with your body then, Paul?' Nikki asked seriously.

His face wore a frown of recollection as he rubbed his hands self-consciously over the matrix of scars under his ribs. They were not, in his mind, badges of honour. More like memories of horror. 'Ah well, those war stories are for another day.' He looked at her fondly. 'I'm off to get the coffee and the daily news.'

The Argentinean grenades in the Falklands had left an untidy series of three scar-ridges, low down on his right abdomen below his rib cage. In Berlin the German's 9mm bullet had torn its way upwards from below his heart, ripped his lung and lodged in the muscle of his right shoulder. Where the bullet entered was a star of scarred flesh, still reasonably new looking. Just below his right pectoral, between the ribs, was the scar of the emergency cut through his chest into the space between his inner and outer lung linings. His lung had been filling dangerously with blood and had to be emptied. Up on his shoulder were a series of neat crossed incisions, about four inches long, where the brilliant German surgeon had operated to locate the bullet, repair the tissue and nerve damage and tidy him up.

He had nearly died. But that was over two years ago and now he was physically fit, tough in body and mind, but still soft in his soul.

He went out to get coffee and the paper.

* * *

PAUL WALKED DOWN Lupus Street to the area of the junction of Grosvenor Road and Chelsea Bridge. The streets were busy with mid-summer weekday traffic and people movement. He had hastily pulled on a pair of battered shorts, shagged out deck shoes and a T-shirt emblazoned with the Pink Floyd logo, one of the classic rock groups closest to his musical heart, and it was just as well since the day was building up to be a scorcher.

The tourists were starting to gather and move: the area was a magnet to the overseas visitors to London at this time of year. North to the posh shops and bars, south to the River Thames, East to Westminster and West to, well, Chelsea and the King's Road.

Paul headed down to the River where an ex-con, solid London man called Billy Hopkins, ran a small coffee-cum-paper stall on the Embankment at a spot that looked directly onto Battersea Power Station. Paul always went there for his coffee if he could. He liked Billy. He liked the honest verbal exchanges the man always swapped with him. He knew Billy was a crook, well ex-crook turned legit small time trader, and Billy knew Paul was a serious military man, and the two of them had, over a number of years now, divined a certain level of each other's truths and set them as the basis for a casual friendship which included the sharing of gossip and news.

''Morning, Major Paul,' said Billy Hopkins. 'What are you doin' 'ere? Never mind. What'll it be? The usual?'

'No, Billy, two coffees, please.'

'What! Come on, Paul, you 'aven't been doin' the naughty, 'ave you? Got a girlfriend at last? And why aren't you at work this Monday mornin'?'

'I'm on leave, Billy, and no comment.'

'Fuck me, that's unusual for you, Major. Thought you couldn't get enough of the old Ministry of Defence and all the bollocks that goes on inside the place. On leave! Well I never. So why the two coffees, Major?'

'Mine to know and yours to wonder, Billy.'

'Toff! That's a toff's answer, Paul. Come on, spill the beans to Billy.'

'Not on your life, Mr Hopkins. Let's have the coffees. Put them in those take-away cups you have with the lids, please. And I'll take a *Daily Mail* today.'

'Now I'm seriously worried, Paul. The *Mail*? You've always been a *Telegraph* man since ever I've known you.'

'Well I'm not today. The DT is not for when I'm on leave, only for work. You know how it is, Billy, you've got to set the perceptions of your superiors if you need to advance in life. And my superiors in the old MOD, as you call it, are a mixture of brilliant and totally dull. They mostly, though, read the *Daily Telegraph*; therefore so do I. Call me shallow and it's true. But I do like the crossword. My Dad and I used to do it before he died.'

'But today it's the bleedin' *Mail* because you've shacked up with some girl and you're on leave and you wants a light read. Is that it?'

'Correct,' Paul said, and let his answer hang tantalisingly in the air between the two of them as his thoughts returned fleetingly to the growing love in his life that was Nikki Walker-Haig. He watched Billy prepare his coffees and one for himself.

'So, serious now, Paul, who is the undoubtedly lovely lady who seems at short notice to 'ave entered your life?' Hopkins turned towards Paul and asked the question with a concerned proprietorial look on his face, as he placed two Styrofoam cups of coffee on the small counter of his booth. 'You want sugar, Paul?'

'No thanks, Billy.'

'Come on then, mate, what's 'er name and what's 'er game?'

'Nikki. And if I tell you any more and you blow the gaff on me, Billy, I'll have to kill you, you realise this don't you?' And although there wasn't a trace of seriousness in Paul's tone, it was as if Billy Hopkins took what he knew of Paul's soldiering background to heart.

'Swear to God, Paul, nothin' will slip my lips,' he said gravely.

'She's over from Nepal…'

'That's the old Gurkha country ain't it?' Hopkins interrupted, happy to change the subject.

'Yes, Billy, it is. I used to be one of them. And as I was saying, she's over in London on business and we've just somehow got together.'

'Pull the other one, my friend, 'fings like that don't just 'appen.'

'Well they do. She's got business meetings this week and then she's got some time off before she goes back. She called me at the office.'

'So 'ow come she 'ad your number then?' Hopkins interrupted Paul.

'No idea. Must have looked it up and made enquiries,' Paul mumbled slightly. He'd wondered himself about how exactly Nikki had tracked him down. But he wasn't surprised. He knew her to be a resourceful woman. Finding him had been no problem to her and Danny Dalloway would have told her where he lived and worked. 'Anyway,' he said, 'she came

126

over last week, spent some time with her elder sister down in the Weymouth area, I think, and now she's here, just for a few days.'

Billy smiled at him. 'Well I'm pleased for yer, Paul, I really am. It fuckin' gladdens my 'eart to see you takin' some time off and talkin' about somethin' normal like a girl. Good on yer.'

'Thanks, Billy. Now what about the paper?'

''Ere it is. Not much in the 'eadlines today. Seems like this fuckin' 'eatwave is all the press can talk about. Well that and the Government. Maggie's under pressure from that bleedin' stupid Poll Tax malarkey up in Scotland.' Hopkins handed the paper to Paul. 'Tell you somethin' I did notice, Paul.'

'What's that, Billy?' Paul took the paper, folded it under his arm and picked up the two coffees. He needed to get back home.

'Look at it when you get 'ome. It's on page four. Just a small column item in amongst them bits about what 'appened this day ten years ago. You know the stuff. Well, it's about the Great Train Robbery, in which I've always 'ad an abiding interest, so to speak.'

'How so?'

'Well, the blokes what done it weren't seriously bad crooks like they were sometimes made out to be, if you get my drift. And since they was all released, I've bumped into one or two of 'em.' Paul frowned slightly. This was a new side to Billy Hopkins. He was genuinely intrigued.

'Tell me more. But make it quick. The coffee cools.'

'You know about it, Paul?'

'Yes, but only from what's been said publicly and from what my parents talked about at the time.'

It was The Crime Of The Century. 1963. Something like two point six million pounds of small denomination bank notes stolen from the Mail Train on its run from Glasgow to London. The heist, hard on the heels of the Profumo Affair, had somehow tortured the conscience and affronted the stewardship of the Harold MacMillan Government, to the extent that even the judiciary felt it had to hand down savage prison sentences for what was essentially an unarmed robbery. Some of the Robbers had escaped from prison, most notoriously, Ronnie Biggs, but for the remainder, the severity of the sentences had been appealed against and they had been out of prison for a long time now.

'Well,' said Hopkins, 'I knew Buster Edwards, for a start, one of the planners, and Charlie Wilson, 'e was the paymaster. When Buster got out 'e became a retailer like me, after a while. Sold flowers at Waterloo Station. Still doin' it.' Hopkins sipped at his own coffee and the reflective expression on his face betokened a fall back into the past. Paul wasn't sure he wanted nor had the time or patience right now to get embroiled in one of Billy Hopkins's long-winded stories. He needn't have worried. Hopkins's face straightened as he looked into Paul's eyes.

'Anyway, the bloke what helped set it all up, the Robbery, like, was this chap called Brian Field. 'E was a good mate of Buster's, as well, as it 'appened. Got Buster off the 'ook for a prior job. Anways it was Brian Field who bollocksed the clean up after the robbery at that farmhouse place near Oakley in Bucks and supposedly made off with more than 'is fair share of the cash.' Hopkins sipped more of his coffee.

Paul made to go. 'So what's the mystery, Billy?'

'Field was released like they all was,' said Billy, 'and changed his name and his life. 'Cept no one knew this, nor 'is new identity, 'til he was killed in a car crash. It 'appened in April seventy-nine but it took the authorities 'til the third of July that year to establish that one of the blokes killed in that crash, who was called Brian Carlton, was actually Brian Field the disappeared Robber. Ten years ago today, it was.' Hopkins smiled and looked relieved. 'Anyway, Paul, it's in the paper, as I said. Just a bit 'o interest for folks like me.'

Paul took his leave and started back to his flat. He couldn't help but think about what Billy Hopkins had said and he dimly recalled the papers and gossip at this time, ten years ago, but only dimly. He was in the final throes of SAS Selection, Officer Week, and was about to be awarded the coveted SAS sand-coloured beret. He was also about to be posted as a troop commander in A Squadron, 22 SAS, so he'd had much on his mind and hadn't paid attention to the revelations he'd heard talked about of Brian Carlton's true identity.

He put the matter out of his mind as he approached Lupus Street and his flat. He had the coffees and the paper and he was on leave and falling in love with a wonderful woman.

But what he didn't know was that Brian Field, the Great Train Robber, had just entered his life.

12

LOVE AND FATE

'I THINK I'M in love with you,' he said. He had found her in the kitchen, which was at the end of the hallway.

'Wow, Stanton, that's quite a statement when you've only been out to buy coffee and the paper.' Nikki was naked, standing against the kitchen sink. She turned to face him. 'Is it anything to do with the fact that I have no clothes on and I'm gorgeous?' The comment might have been a touch flip but her face was serious. Her hair was tied back in a bunch with an old bootlace she had found somewhere amongst his bits and pieces. She was unaffected, utterly comfortable in her own skin and totally stunning.

'No,' he replied. He tried to focus his thoughts and explain to himself why he had suddenly come out with such life-changing words. 'The coffee might need a boost of heat. Billy Hopkins was banging on to me endlessly, which is why I'm a little late in getting back.' Paul lamely handed the two Styrofoam cups to her and placed the paper on the side. 'And I have been thinking about it.' He leaned towards her, took her face gently in his hands and kissed her softly.

'About what?' She breathed out, her chest was heaving. 'Phew, you really have some effect on me, Paul.'

'Good. About the fact that I love you: it's not a spur of the moment thing.'

'Of course it is. We've only been properly introduced for four days. I wasn't meant to be in London at this time but here I am. Danny gave me your number and I called you out of the blue because you'd failed to come back out to Kathmandu as promised. I gate-crashed your tidy little flat and the spare bedroom wasn't going to be an option, because I needed you.' Nikki ran out of steam and stood helpless looking at Paul. Then she recovered herself, found a small saucepan in the pan cupboard and sparked one of the gas rings. She poured the coffees into the pan, got out two mugs from one of the cupboards and a spoon and watched the coffee start to simmer. 'And who is Billy Hopkins?' she said, changing the subject and regaining some semblance of composure.

Paul wasn't to be deflected. 'I'll tell you in a minute. So what do you think?'

'Take your T-shirt off and give it to me. I might set fire to myself otherwise.' Paul dutifully obliged. 'What I think is that I'll just warm the coffee up and then we can add a dop of something uplifting and mind-cleansing. Some of your Gurkha rum should do it, if you have any, or brandy? Sounds like we might need some emotional and physical reinforcements here, Paul. And you are on leave after all and it does sound as if the road ahead just got a touch uncertain.'

'Why?'

'Because I think I'm in love with you, too.'

And that was that.

* * *

THEY WERE SIDE-BY-SIDE on the sofa in his sitting room. There was also an armchair, a small TV, two bookcases of precious books, his fairly state-of-the-art hi-fi system stacked on a lovely oak chest and some old wooden crates which housed his cherished long playing records. The prints on the walls were few and tasteful. The window was wide open but the air was hot and now getting humid.

They had drunk their coffee, laced with brandy. Now they sipped glasses of chilled white wine. They were relaxed in the situation they had both declared to each other. It would change their lives, but neither had a real clue as to how much and when, and how the changes might manifest themselves. Although it would be sooner than either would think possible

'This is a lovely flat, Paul,' Nikki said.

'It is,' he replied.

'How long have you had it?'

'I bought it six years ago.' His was a two-bedroom flat on the top, third, floor in a terrace, Number 17 Lupus Street, Pimlico, London.

'You did the right thing.'

Paul looked at Nikki and saw the happiness in her face and his feelings mirrored hers. He couldn't remember when he'd felt so contented and at ease. His life had been uncertain and dangerous for too long and he needed some stability and love. He decided to tell her about himself. He felt this woman was going to be a large part of his future and needed to know about him.

'Well, I'd spent so much time on operations that somehow I'd managed to save enough for the deposit. My Mum helped me with the furnishings.' He gestured at the curtains, carpet and the pictures on the walls, and his arm waved back down towards the hallway. 'Not too bachelor-esque, I hope, nor overbearingly military? I needed a refuge and a shelter.'

'No. It's really lovely, and it suits you.'

Paul looked at Nikki and detected a hint of nostalgia or regret in the fine lines of her face. 'What's up?'

'Nothing, honestly, but I'm envious, and I wish I had something as solid as this to show for my life's work but I never achieved it,' she replied. 'Too much waste in my previous relationship, and now I'm working with Danny Dalloway on his project, which as you know is only just getting off the ground, so the chances of me ever being in this sort of position are pretty slim.' She turned towards him and smiled without any trace of rancour or jealousy. 'Have you told many women that you love them in this home of yours, Stanton?' And Nikki Walker-Haig chuckled teasingly as she said it.

'Truth? No. None. There has never been another woman who has slept in the bed.' And it was the truth. He'd never really tried.

'Not even when you were not on operations?' Nikki wasn't teasing him now and Paul knew it. It was obviously important for her to know the man she was with. No secrets.

'No secrets. My Dad always banged on about having a property, even if it was tiny, which this is. So I took the plunge after the Falklands.' He sipped his wine. 'The irony is that my Dad died before that particular war so he never saw the place. He never saw lots of things.'

'I knew that, Paul. Danny told me and I'm ever so sorry. I'm sure your Dad would have been very proud of you.'

'Maybe. Maybe. Yes, I think he would have. Anyway,' Paul said wistfully, 'the flat was my refuge when I was at Staff College during the leave breaks and when I could get here up the A30 some weekends. The mortgage payments were manageable and still are. When I went to the Gurkhas I didn't have to rent it out. I'm fantastically lucky: a single major earning Special Forces pay.' Paul challenged Nikki with a knowing look. 'And I never really had a girlfriend or a lavish lifestyle.'

'Never? Come on, Paul, what about the woman called Christina that Danny and some of the Gurkhas were talking about in Kathmandu?'

Paul felt glad that Nikki had raised the subject. She had to know. 'You heard what happened, I'm guessing. Danny must have told you. He certainly told everyone else when I was in Nepal,' and Paul laughed a little. 'That man could never keep a secret.' Then he got serious again. 'Danny was very good to us both, and to me afterwards.'

'Did you love her?'

'Yes I did, or thought I did; but the feeling was totally different from what I feel now, so I suppose it wasn't true love.' He leaned towards Nikki and his expression was quizzical. 'You know what I mean, Nik? You must have felt the same for your partner, the one you almost married. You must have thought you loved him.' Paul sat back against the cushions and his voice took on a reflective tone. 'I don't have a predatory, one-night-stand nature as far as women are concerned. If anything I'm parsimonious with my emotions. I believe in love and romance, the old-fashioned ways underpinned by moral truth.' He looked at her again and he was deadly serious. He felt good telling her these innermost thoughts. 'Only when I find true feelings do I commit. Which was how I thought I wanted to be with Christina, if that makes any sense.'

'It does,' she said.

'But I have a terrible side to me and Christina couldn't handle it. Despite being an MI5 researcher and working in that Godforsaken place called Northern Ireland, she couldn't handle it. No secrets?'

'No secrets, Paul,' Nikki answered him.

'Well you know of it, anyway, but you don't know the stark-staring, brutal reality of what happened. Christina did because she saw it and lived alongside it for months. I kill people. I kill bad people: those that I'm ordered to kill and those that threaten me, my beliefs and those I love or have a duty to protect. Like you, now.' Paul got up. 'I need another drink,' he said, the emotion obvious in his voice.

He wandered through to the kitchen, pulled the wine bottle from the fridge and came back. He filled up Nikki's glass and sat back down in the chair across from her, bottle in one hand, glass in the other. 'In the dark days after my soldiers were killed in Northern Ireland, Christina was one of my lifelines. She faced the dangers of being with me on a deniable operation, sanctioned by the PM of course, but deniable nonetheless. We ended up in West Berlin's Wall Zone, via Bandit Country, West Belfast and the South of Ireland. It was a long, tough journey. She was incredibly brave. I had to kill three men. I'm not proud of it, but they'd crossed the line where forgiveness is not an option. They all had to die.'

'They had to?'

'They did, and the last of these killings Christina witnessed. Others were killed at the same time. She was there, a main player in a really dangerous game to expose the truth and get the Army and the Government off the hook.' Paul drank again and got up and sat down beside her. Nikki put her hand on his thigh and he felt the warm tenderness of it. 'Actually it got me off the hook as well.'

'How so?'

'Well my career was ruined. I was a disgraced Army officer. The operation allowed all of us to return from the shadows, Her Majesty's Government as well, although that would be denied by everyone. But it was all too much for her and I understand it. I got shot by a big German bastard and it very nearly did for me. Christina helped save my life.'

'Oh, Paul.'

He was conscious that he was talking too much about the past and needed to bring things back to the present, because Paul Stanton wasn't much interested in the past. He was interested only in Nikki Walker-Haig and the feelings he had for her.

'Yeah, it was touch and go for a while. Christina had witnessed it all. Anyway', Paul said, 'we tried to make a go of it afterwards, but it didn't work. My violent craft, the pulls it has on me and what it makes me, were too much for her.'

'She was a brave woman, Paul, and I respect her for trying to love you. I'm glad she's gone from your life though. Is that horrible of me?'

'No. It's the loveliest thing anyone has ever said to me. And no, she never came here. And I've been a solitary man ever since. But now I've met you and I don't want to lose you.'

'I'm not going anywhere except to make us a sandwich. Come with me and help because I'm starving and nervous and slightly drunk and very, very happy, Major Stanton!'

'Christ,' Paul exclaimed. 'I've totally forgotten to tell you something really important.'

'What?'

'They're going to promote me. Make me a Lieutenant Colonel. The list was published last Friday. You turning up here made me forget about it.'

'Wow, Stanton, that's impressive. What does it mean exactly?'

'What does it mean? Lots of possibilities. I'll be in the rank and paid this time next year but I could get an early posting as an Acting-something, in which case they'd have to pay me as well, and it's quite a pay hike, so worth it. But who knows? I don't sit and plan and think about these things, Nik, as I suspect you know. But it's good news. It means I am now a totally rehabilitated serving officer in her Majesty's Army for the foreseeable future.'

'Well in that case I'll stick with you, Stanton. Come on we need grub.'

* * *

IN THE SNUG room off the kitchen there was a small fold out table with two chairs. The snug was Paul's den and in addition to the table it had a battered old comfy chair in it, more books and a reading lamp. When he was at home it was where he often liked to end the day with a good read and a dram. He and Nikki were chatting, munching and Paul was flicking idly through the *Daily Mail*.

'And here's another thing that slipped out of my feeble mind. Page four of the *Daily Mail*, Monday the third of July nineteen eighty-nine.'

'Mmm? Today. So what?' Nikki looked at him.

'I told you about Billy Hopkins, the coffee and paper man, didn't I?'

'Sort of,' she responded.

'He's an ex-con with some serious gangster friends from the annals of British criminal activity.'

'What!' Nikki's face took on a quizzical look.

'Yes, some of the Great Train Robbers for a start, two of the main men, Charlie Wilson, for example, and Buster Edwards who now sells flowers outside Waterloo Station. Anyway, Billy told me there was an interest piece in the *Mail* today about one of the Great Train Robbers, which there is. It's in the what-happened-ten-years-ago-today item.'

'And what did happen ten years ago today?'

'Well one of the Great Train Robbers, Brian Field, was identified as one of the victims in a car crash on the M4 Motorway. The crash actually happened on the twenty-seventh of April nineteen seventy-nine, whilst I, you might be interested to know was being eaten alive by jungle creatures in Brunei.'

'Ouch. More fool you, Stanton.'

'I shall ignore that. Brian Field was living under an assumed name so his real identity wasn't established until the third of July, ten years ago today. It took the authorities that long because no one claimed his body, so they had to trace back through his dental records to identify his birth name. The problem was that everyone in the crash was killed. Two cars were involved.'

'Dear God, Paul, that sounds horrendous.'

'It was, apparently, and utterly improbable. There was a family in the other car. The daughter of Raymond Bessone, the famous hairdresser, and her husband and their two children. The woman was pregnant, too.' Nikki was speechless. Paul went on. 'Brian Field and his young wife Sian were in the other car. All six people were killed instantly. Bessone's daughter's car hit the crash barrier and torpedoed into Field's car coming up on the other side of the motorway. Imagine it.'

'I can't,' Nikki said.

'Anyway, the point of the story is that when he was killed Brian Field was living, and married, under the name of Carlton. The man killed was Brian Carlton but he was really Brian Field the Great Train Robber.'

'I don't believe it!' Nikki exclaimed. 'Are you sure?'

'Yes. Here,' and Paul pushed the *Mail* across to Nikki so she could read it for herself. Which she did and then turned to Paul with a mixture of surprise and worry on her face.

'My big sister knew Brian Carlton.'

But before Paul could respond, the telephone on the hallway table started ringing. 'Who knows you're here, Nik?' Paul asked. The call was unlikely to be for him. No one ever called him at home - excepting his mother, and she wouldn't be calling at this time on a Monday.

'Only my sister,' she answered. 'I had to give her your number. It was the only contact number I had. I told her to ring here if she was in trouble or needed help. Do you mind?'

'No, of course not.' He went to answer the 'phone but he knew it wasn't for him. It would be Nikki's older sister.

It was. And her voice sounded strained.

Paul suddenly had that feeling of the fates shifting and drawing him by mysterious forces into something completely unplanned, unlikely and unforeseen. It was a feeling he had grown to trust over the years for it had never let him down nor disappointed him. Although he had a deeply ingrained yearning for adventure and action he suddenly wasn't sure the uncertainty of such situations was what he wanted right now.

He handed the telephone handset to Nikki and left her to talk to her sister.

13

THE ROSE & CROWN

NIKKI CAME OFF the 'phone in a state of agitation. She told Paul her sister was in London and sounded really upset, and had asked them to meet her at a pub in Kew Green, close to where she used to live.

'What's it about, Nik?'

'She thinks she's being stalked and is very frightened. Let me get ready and I'll tell you more when we're on the move. She shouldn't even be in London 'til later today, so something's spooked her badly.'

'OK. Where in Kew Green?'

'The Rose & Crown pub.'

Paul Stanton wasn't a man to waste time speculating about things he would find out about soon enough, especially when they had to get moving, so as Nikki went off to dress he filled a water bottle and put it into a small daysack along with a tatty old sunhat and a thin well-worn Egyptian cotton jumper. He made sure he had sunglasses, money, ID, his pocket A-Z and house keys, and secured the flat's windows. Nikki was ready in less than five minutes. She was wearing a loose cotton shirt and shorts, had some scuffed sandals on her feet and held a lightweight cardigan in her hand. Paul stuffed it into the daysack. She looked stunning with Ray Bans crammed onto her head and locked firmly in place by her lustrous hair.

They made the journey to Kew Bridge station and walked south crossing the Thames towards Kew Green. They had been quiet on the journey, just making sure they made the right underground and overland tube and train connections and knew where they were going. They walked purposefully.

'My sister's a freelance wildlife photographer and journalist. Quite well known and frequently on assignment for *National Geographic*, *Wildlife* and such-like,' Nikki said. They were holding hands and looked like any other romantic couple strolling in the south London sun on a fine July afternoon. Except that Nikki Walker-Haig was tense. Paul could feel it.

'And you said she's down in Weymouth and you stayed with her last week?'

'Yes. Portland actually. That's her home when she's not away on assignment. But she's also occasionally up here and has a bed whenever she needs it in her old flat, which she sold some years ago to a work colleague. It's just down the road from the pub we're going to.'

'OK,' Paul replied, 'well we're not far away.' They were coming onto the bridge and Paul knew that once across they had to turn right in order to find the road for the pub. 'So is there anything else I should know before I meet her?' He felt a slight tremor in her body and so stopped her gently by the arm, turned to face her, tilted up her sunglasses and studied the concern in her sparkling eyes. 'You said she's very frightened, and in my book that's serious. You said she thought she was being stalked, which I don't like the sound of at all. So what's going on? I need to know if I'm going to help.'

Nikki sighed and relaxed, holding on to his arm as they stood for a few minutes and talked.

'Victoria, Vikki, is off on assignment to the Sudan tomorrow to photograph some threatened Sudanese Oryx apparently, at the request of the Saharan Conservation Fund.' Paul watched her closely. There was something not right about this. Nikki went on. 'She was planning to come up to London today because she flies tomorrow from Heathrow. But she told me she'd driven up to London late Saturday night because she was too scared to stay in her cottage in Portland. She said she was worried about her safety. And it's all happened since I left there on Thursday.'

'What exactly's happened?' Paul asked her.

'She didn't say much. Just that it was about some really dodgy-looking men at home who were after her and that she had to get away. It's not like her, Paul. She's scared and she doesn't scare easily, my tough outdoor sister.' Nikki hesitated. 'There's something else, Paul.'

'Concerning Brian Carlton?' Paul asked. 'To do with that newspaper item?' He had been wondering when the two of them would get back to the subject they'd been talking about before the telephone call had galvanized them into action.

'Yes. I don't know very much of the detail, but I do know that Vikki knew Brian Carlton back in the seventies when she was working out what to do with her life and living here in Kew. Our parents were in Weymouth, but they're not there now. At that time, though, they owned a restaurant, The Spinnaker, and Vikki would come home every now and then and regale us with her wondrous stories of the glamour life of working in London and travelling to European cities and all that.'

'OK.'

'It was the middle of nineteen seventy-eight when she first told us that she was working with someone called Brian Carlton. He and his wife Sian lived in the same block of flats as Vikki, just down the road from the pub we're going to. That's how she met them. They even came to Weymouth, stayed with our parents and ate in the restaurant. That's a weird coincidence, isn't it?'

'It is,' he said with a detectable trace of anticipation in his tone. 'So let's go and meet her. We'll have to see how we can help her, won't we?' Paul's antennae were finely tuned and he was beginning to feel that whatever the threat to Victoria might be, the timing, the anniversary of Brian Carlton's death, *was* too much of a coincidence. He didn't trust coincidence.

They started walking again.

'Thank you, Paul; I knew it would be all right with you here. I'm afraid I already told her that you're in the SAS. Are you angry?'

'Of course not,' he said, squeezing her hand. It was what he did: protecting those threatened by bad forces. But what forces? And how could they be connected with a Great Train Robber who'd been dead for ten years? He needed more information and he might need help; but he'd decide on exactly what after he'd met and talked to Victoria Walker-Haig.

* * *

THE ROSE & CROWN was a lovely pub, nineteen-thirties or forties built, Paul guessed, with blackened exposed beams on its frontage, bricked and white-painted and fit for all-seasons' hospitality. Its three sets of chimneys would carry smoke from its welcoming fires in the winter days when folk sought the warmth of log and coal fires; but today its outside seating areas with tables and sun umbrellas were perfect for a hot summer's day.

The pub's aspect overlooked Kew Green with its cricket pavilion and immaculate square. There would have been a local match played on this ground yesterday, for certain. At the end of the road were the wrought iron gates of Kew Botanical Gardens. Behind the pub was the River Thames with a towpath. Paul was instantly comfortable in such a place. It was very English, a perfect summer scene, yet, paradoxically, it was connected in some way to the unpredictability of English criminal activity.

The three of them were sitting on the top level of outdoor seating. Whilst steps gave access to the lower area at road level, Paul had chosen a table on the upper terrace with its seats backed against the brick exterior of the pub. From here he could see all the movement of people walking past the frontage and coming and going from the pub's doors. There was just the outside chance that Victoria might have been followed here from Portland. So far, though, everything was unremarkable.

Paul wore his sunhat, which shaded his eyes sufficiently for him to see the changing emotions in Victoria's face and eyes. She was talking quietly and was evidently very worried. Paul could see it plainly. It showed in touches of nervousness in her body language as well.

He had liked her instantly, but she was nothing like her sister. Nikki was close to five foot eight in height, with burnt-brown hair, sparkling mint chocolate coloured eyes and an oval face with finely cut nose and mouth. She was slim, fit, and beautiful. Her sister was of a similar height but with dirty blond colouring and bluey eyes. The exigencies of her work had given her what he could only think of as an outdoor complexion. She appeared to be no-nonsense and functional in her appearance and approach, not unattractive, far from it, clearly fit with an athletic tone to her body, but not his type. She was nice.

They were drinking long glasses of weak Pimm's with plenty of fruit and ice. Paul had instructed the barman to make it to his exact requirements. They all needed refreshment and clear heads. Just a trace of alcohol would help.

Victoria started to explain why she left Portland in such a hurry. Her thoughts were all over the place. She then asked: 'Don't you think I sound a touch paranoid, Paul?'

'No, I don't.' In his lifetime's experience intelligent rational and balanced people did not suffer from paranoia. Mostly such people discovered good cause for their concerns, whether deep-rooted or superficial. He sipped his drink. But he needed to get a handle on what was really happening. There would be signposts in this story if he listened closely and asked the right questions, but so far the detail he needed was incomplete.

'I'm not surprised you were scared,' Nikki joined in. 'You believe men have been watching your cottage and stalking you?'

'I do believe it, yes. You know the cottage area, Nikki, and normally it's impossible for strangers not to stand out. The place is too small for newcomers not to be noticed. They were in the Cove as well.'

'The Cove?' Paul asked. 'A beach, a pub name? And you said normally.'

'It's a pub close to my cottage,' Victoria answered. 'My local and small, right on that part of Chesil Beach with a fantastic sunset at this time of the year. Normally strangers stand out like beacons in the night, except in high summer when the place can be really crowded with all sorts, which is now, of course. However, these two men I'm talking of, had also been scouting up and down the street and in amongst the cottages and fish sheds. I'd seen them and thought at the time that they didn't look like tourists.'

'How not?' Paul asked.

'I don't know. They weren't dressed like summer holidaymakers. They had a purpose behind what they were doing and they didn't look happy and relaxed.' Which was good enough for Paul. If Victoria's instincts rang her alarm bells then he trusted them to be right. She went on. 'I was mostly indoors, but popped out now and then to get to the shops. I was working on my last project that had to be submitted today, and of course getting myself ready for the trip tomorrow.' She paused. 'And then they came into the Cove. They watched me the whole time.'

'When was this?' asked Nikki anxiously. 'After I left, obviously, so it must have been Friday?'

'Friday and Saturday,' Victoria answered. 'Fortunately I was with friends. But seeing these men unnerved me and so I decided to get away and stay in the old flat. Melanie's not here and I have a key as you know.' Paul needed to get some chronology and definition into this story. The girls were dotting around inside a loop of understanding and physical landscapes he knew nothing about.

'What exactly happened, Vikki?'

'Later on Saturday night, after the Cove incident, I went into my kitchen to get a last drink and saw a man in the dark, looking through the window. I'm sure it was one of them. No one could be there accidentally, so I knew they really were after me.'

'How scary,' said Nikki, holding her sister's hand.

'It was. I was really shaken. The light was off, thankfully. Whoever was there rattled the back door handle and then I heard the person moving away towards the street.'

'Why didn't you call the Police?' Nikki asked. Good question, Paul said to himself.

'I don't know. I never thought of it. Anyway, I waited for about fifteen minutes, packed up all my stuff for the Sudan trip and jumped in the car while there were still people around leaving the pubs and chip shops. I drove up here. I'm exhausted.' She sipped her drink and looked bleakly at Paul. 'There was something else?'

'What was that?'

'The landlady in the Cove told me that the two men I'd seen in the pub were foreign. Their English was very good, apparently, but with a trace of an accent, possibly German. She also said they didn't sound and act like holidaymakers and had been asking questions about where I lived.'

Germans? Paul was now totally intrigued. Germans and Great Train Robbers? How so? He topped up the girls' Pimms glasses. Nikki's hand rested on his thigh and her fingers stroked him absentmindedly. He was convinced that Victoria's safety was under threat but had no idea how it was or could be even remotely connected to the Great Train Robber story.

'Tell me about Brian Carlton, Vikki, from the beginning if you would, please. Then I might be able to help you.'

So Victoria Walker-Haig did; and it was one of the most fascinating and improbable stories he had ever heard.

14

VICTORIA'S STORY

'IT WAS NINETEEN seventy-eight and I was living here, in Kew Green, just down the road from this pub, number twenty-seven, the second floor flat. I was renting it while trying to find some permanent work after a series of misguided adventures in tourism and teaching in Spain.' Victoria's expression was reflective and a smile played around her mouth. These were obviously fond memories for her. 'They were good times.'

'In what way,' Paul asked.

'Well I met Brian Carlton for a start. And I ended up buying the flat.'

'As a result of your friendship with Carlton?' Paul queried.

'I suppose so; but only because he paid me well over the ten months or so that I worked for him, and I was able to save my wages. Eventually, a couple of years later I had enough to put down the deposit to buy the flat and pay the mortgage. But it was more than that. It was a slightly crazy and very exciting life for those months and we travelled, boy did we travel and had lots of real fun, but then he and Sian were killed.' Her voice trailed away and she took a drink. Her eyes were sparkling with a trace of tears. Nikki leaned across and squeezed her sister's hand. 'I liked them both very much but her more so than him, and I think I was the only person other than Sian's family maybe, who grieved for him after the crash. No one seemed to know Brian. Now of course I know why.'

'Let's order a sandwich or something,' said Paul, handing one of the table's menu cards to the two women. 'I'll place the order. I'm famished and you girls must be, too.' Nikki and Victoria told him their preferences and he went into the bar, ordered and paid. The interior was busy with tourist couples and families, and some business people with customers or colleagues. There was nothing that struck Paul as out of the ordinary. No Germans, at least.

Within ten minutes they were all eating and talking once more. Victoria continued her story.

'I was in this very pub one night, about this time of year because I'd completed my post grad course in journalism, when this ordinary looking guy came in accompanied by a tall and most beautiful blonde woman. He had a brisk manner about him, rounded features, longish sandy-coloured hair, thinning slightly. I remember everything about the two of them. He always wore blue corduroy trousers and a blue shirt or jumper. He was quite smooth and well mannered, but he was in contrast to Sian who was absolutely beautiful and must have been fifteen years younger than him. She had the most perfect skin I've ever seen.'

Victoria took another forkful of her chicken salad and chewed thoughtfully. 'I recognised her because I'd seen her before; we'd bumped into one another in the entrance hallway of the building. Sian and Brian lived in the downstairs flat.'

'And what happened next is the really interesting thing, Paul,' said Nikki, who obviously knew the story. 'Go on, Vikki, tell Paul,' she insisted.

'Well we introduced ourselves, so I knew he was Brian Carlton. We started talking over a drink and Brian asked me about my background and education and he told me about the business he worked in, which was something called the Children's Book Centre based out of offices in Kensington High Street. He was responsible for the south and central Europe operations.'

'And Vikki ended up working for him!' Nikki couldn't contain herself. Paul smiled at her and felt a surge of affection course through him. She'd lost the potentially serious import of the situation in the excitement of sharing her sister's extraordinary story.

'How did that happen?' Paul asked.

'I remember what Brian Carlton said: "Do you have a job at the moment and if you don't would you like one?" I said yes, of course! He then asked if I had a passport and if I could drive a transit van. "Very well," I replied, "I've been delivering fish and eggs to Pontins and other places all along the south coast for ages for my Dad in his vans." "Good," he said, "because I've got a transit van loaded with books for a book exhibition in the International School in Brussels this week and I need a driver and someone competent enough to set

152

it all up and sell books. Are you up for it?" And without waiting for my reply he said: "If you are then please stop drinking now because you're booked on the six forty-five ferry from Dover to Ostend tomorrow morning. Think you can do it? And this is the address of the school," and he gave me this piece of paper, "and the van is already loaded and parked outside the house. You're covered on the insurance. I'll expect you back here, with the cash that you make fully accounted for in five days. The School will fix your accommodation and it's paid for up front. And here's some cash for your expenses and food. It's yours." He handed me an envelope full of banknotes and that's almost exactly how it all started.'

Paul shook his head slowly. 'That's some story, Vikki!'

'It is! So I did exactly what he asked and went on from there.' Victoria finished off the remnants of her lunch hurriedly.

Paul checked his watch. It was one-thirty. There was more he needed to hear from Victoria about Brian Field, much more, but there were thoughts forming in his mind about what he might need to do, and for these he had to create some time before he could act.

'So if this was summer nineteen seventy-eight,' he said, 'and Carlton was killed in April seventy-nine, were you working for him all this time and what was he like?'

'Yes, I was working for the Book Centre during that period and Brian was my boss. I did exhibitions in Holland, Luxembourg, all over Scandinavia, and during the school holidays worked in the main offices in Kensington High Street. The Book Centre's vehicle depot and book warehouse was down in Camberley and I went down there sometimes.'

Paul asked, 'Did you work alone?'

'No, there were a couple of us but I never did an exhibition with Brian, not until after that Christmas. He tended to deal with the schools and opportunities in Spain. In fact he became good friends with Prince Felipe and his teenage sisters through their English tutor. The International School in Madrid held regular book fairs and Brian and Sian always went and stayed in the finest rooms of the Hotel Aristos.'

'And they came down to visit Mum and Dad and ate in the restaurant in Weymouth as well,' Nikki added. 'I told Paul this.'

'They did, over one long weekend when we had no work on,' she replied.

'So it would appear the Carltons were never short of money,' mused Paul aloud.

'No, they weren't,' Victoria replied. 'He drove a Porsche for a start. And then there was the trip to Switzerland after Christmas.'

'What happened there?'

'Well it was pretty outrageous and quite strange really.' Paul and Nikki said nothing. 'There was a book exhibition and big fair planned at Aiglon College in Switzerland and Brian asked me to accompany him and Sian. Then something really weird happened.

'What was that?' Paul asked.

154

'Well I'd packed my suitcase ready to go the day before because we were leaving very early in the morning and left it in the communal hallway downstairs by their flat. But when I came down the next morning it had disappeared. I remember Brian being really fussed about what this might mean and getting quite angry and rushing us. He said he wasn't happy about having a garden flat with access to the towpath that ran by the Thames.'

'Why, exactly?'

'I think it was because he thought it was another burglary.'

'Another burglary? There had been others?' Paul's interest was truly piqued now but he had a sense of foreboding as well.

'Yes. One other. Before Christmas he and Sian had come back from Italy, left all the cash takings in a bag behind the radiator in their sitting room, gone out for a meal and come back to find the money had been stolen.'

'What?' Paul said.

'It was true; at least that's what he told me. But I noticed towards the end that he was getting more and more nervous about security. Which probably why the disappearance of my suitcase at that time threw him into a bit of a panic. Anyway, we had to get going so I grabbed a few loose things and shared Sian's stuff for the rest. The three of us drove the transit to Switzerland, did the exhibition at Aiglon and then Brian took us skiing in Crans-Montana for three weeks! It was outrageously expensive and he paid for everything.'

As he had suspected, Paul was picking up the little telltales that might lead to the reasons for Victoria's concerns. There was money behind this situation somehow, he was becoming more and more sure of it. Then what Victoria told them next confirmed it for him.

Nikki prompted the end of the story. 'Tell Paul about the time just before they were killed, Vikki.'

'Well, it was April obviously, and by this time I'd been going to the Canaries a lot and making a new set of friends and thinking about alternative work options. I was going to leave the Children's Book Centre. Anyway, as I told you, the incident about my disappearing suitcase on top of the stolen Italian cash had made Brian a bit paranoid about security. He said to me that he was positive the thieves had believed my suitcase to be one of theirs.'

'So Carlton was quite open about possibly being a target for theft or something like that?' Paul asked.

'He never talked about it in quite those terms; but I noticed when I was back here in Kew and doing the odd bit of work for him that he became increasingly anxious about such things. And then there was the final incident before the weekend they were killed.' Paul and Nikki waited for Victoria to gather herself; she clearly remembered it vividly.

'They were going to visit Sian's parents in Cardiff and Sian came up to my flat on the Friday morning in a state of agitation and with a small attaché case in her hand. I remember exactly what she said. "Vikki, I need a real favour, please. Brian's at the office and when he comes back we're leaving for Wales." Sian looked very worried and put the attaché case down on the floor. She said, "He told me to take this case to the bank to put in our safe deposit but I haven't been able to get there and now I'm out of time. He's worried about burglars whilst we're away, as you know. So can I leave it with you? You'll be here won't you, and you'll put it somewhere safe? It is locked and Brian has the key. I'll come and get it back on Monday and then I'll be able to put it in the bank without Brian knowing it's not there yet." I told her I would be and that it would be fine and I'd look after it for them.' Victoria looked at both Paul and Nikki mournfully. 'But they never came back, did they. They were killed in that awful car crash.'

Yes, thought Paul, it's about money. It usually is. But what are the connections today to something that happened ten years ago? It was the attaché case and it might be about Victoria, but possibly not the latter. But who were the people?

He had to ask. 'Did you know Brian Carlton was actually Brian Field, one of the Great Train Robbers?'

'No, I never did. And I'm positive Sian never did either. Not at any time in the ten months I was with them did I ever hear mention of anything to suggest who he had been or that she knew about his past. We spent a lot of time in each other's company at work and socially.'

'And what happened to the attaché case?'

Victoria told them, but in a roundabout way. 'I mentioned that I was starting a new phase of my life in the Canaries when the Carltons were killed. Well I went off there almost straight afterwards. I stored my stuff away in the spare room and rented the flat to Melanie, a work colleague, who's still there. Eventually I sold it to her, although she lets me stay whenever I'm up in Town, but I didn't sell it and move out until about two years later after I'd finished my Canaries stint and been through a bad relationship or two. The usual stuff one does in one's twenties.'

'And the attaché case?' Paul gently probed her again. He needed to get moving, it was gone two o'clock and he wanted to get north of the River and speak to someone - today.

'Well I've never looked for it, but I must still have it somewhere, I suppose.'

Ah, thought Paul, that explains it. Maybe. 'Seriously? And no one's ever asked you about it?'

'No; and I've never thought about it, until now.'

'How so?'

'I was out of the country when Brian Carlton's true identity was made known. I only knew about it because Mum cut the piece out of the paper and sent it to me.' Victoria Walker-Haig paused thoughtfully. 'As I said, I was abroad for about two years and when I eventually returned I sold the flat to Melanie. It had shot up in value and I was able to buy the cottage in Portland where I knew I could concentrate on photographic journalism. I hired a van, loaded up all my gear that had been stored and moved down there. If it's anywhere, the attaché case is probably somewhere in my moldy old attic.'

And that was Victoria's story.

* * *

SO, MUSED PAUL, Victoria was overseas when Brian Field's true identity was revealed and would not have been personally involved in any immediate and subsequent follow-up by Field's ex-gang, if there was one. And because her gear was stored away in the flat *above* where the Carltons lived, who would even have suspected she had been given an attaché case belonging to one of the Great Train Robbers? Did it contain money? Was that what this was all about? And how, in God's name were Germans involved - if indeed they were - *ten years later*?

Paul needed to get moving and thankfully Victoria was going to the Sudan so would be out of harm's way. Nikki had some business meetings this week and could stay in his flat in Pimlico where she would also be out of things. He had to be free to move and act and he had to go to Portland. Victoria would give him the keys to her cottage and he'd make it his base. He was damned well going to roust out the Germans; but he had to do so before they felt the trail was cold and disappeared.

He was going to Portland, via a nice cosy chat with Billy Hopkins. He needed to eliminate some of the suspects. And he needed to get his car on the road.

15

THE GREAT TRAIN ROBBERS

PAUL HAD LEFT Nikki safe in his flat. He had the keys to Victoria's Portland cottage, a map of where it was and his car was parked up on the Embankment a hundred yards away. He was good to go and should be in Portland in time for an evening drink in the Cove Inn.

He and Nikki had agreed the plan. She had a couple of important business meetings with MozLon in the City on Thursday, or her mission to London would fail and Danny Dalloway's business project would crash and burn.

'Nik, you must focus on the meeting with MozLon's Head of Security, Mr Etherington,' he'd said. 'I'll be back before the weekend, God willing.'

She was realistic enough to see these were her priorities and besides, if there was to be any dark business ahead, then it was best Paul was left to manage it without her in the way. She knew this. She'd been in Kathmandu and had heard all about the Hungarians. He needed to be on his own and she'd understood it.

So Paul had packed his old grip with some essential lightweight clothes and summer outdoor gear and driven the short distance down to the Embankment close to Billy Hopkins' stall. It was three-thirty and he wanted to be on the road to the southwest before the commuter exodus from London started in earnest. He had at least a four-hour drive ahead of him.

'Tell me about the Great Train Robbers, Billy.'

'What! You're jokin', Paul. More than what I already told you this mornin'? It's old news, Major.'

'I know it is, Billy. But tell me about the men involved. Tell me about the ones who would be interested in Brian Field. Where are they now? Dead? Too old for action? Abroad? Come on, Billy, time is against me and you need to tell me stuff. I've got to get on the road. And I don't have the time to pop in and chat with your old mate Buster Edwards either. So you'll have to tell me what I need to know.'

'Cor, fuckin' 'ell, Paul, you're all a bit stiff and arsey of a sudden 'ain't you? No offence intended, mind, Major.'

'None taken, Billy, but it's like this: having been told about the ten-years-ago-today story by you, I've suddenly developed an interest in it and you're the man to tell me.'

They were sitting on portable stools that Hopkins brought to his stall every day. It was almost his packing up time and the shutters were pulled down. They were unlikely to be disturbed. Paul wanted to get to the point, but he needed to be cautious, to a degree, because he couldn't get on the road to Portland without the information he believed Hopkins could give him.

'Billy, how long have you known me?'

161

'You've been comin' 'ere on and off for more than five years, mate,' Hopkins replied. 'I value your trade, Paul, serious I do.'

'And what do you know about me, Billy?'

'Not much, Paul, only the little bits 'an pieces I've sniffed out from the papers and all that, and from gossip in the pubs. That fuckin' great IRA attack on your boys down in Bandit Country back in eighty-five told us all a lot. Then there was the Falklands before that. No, Paul, we all know you're a bleedin' 'ero and that you're in the SAS. Fuck me, mate, that's serious shit that is. You must be tough as old boots and a danger to us all.'

Paul couldn't tell whether or not Hopkins was taking the piss with that last statement, but Billy's face told him he wasn't trying to be smart. The man seemed to understand there was something unusual about this conversation and was being as honest as his brain could marshal his thoughts.

'So, Billy, you wouldn't mess with me then?'

'Fuck off, Major! 'Course I wouldn't. But you're not goin' to ask me to do somethin' dodgy and likely to get me pinched by the fuzz are you?'

'No, Billy. But you have to see that I'm serious and no matter how mad my questions might seem I need you to tell me all you know. OK? And it's going to take no longer than thirty minutes, tops.'

'Fire away, Paul, I'll give you all I got. So it's about the Great Train Robbers you say, well I'll rack my brains for you, that's guaranteed.'

'Who were the main Robbers connected with Brian Field and why would any of them be interested in him now, after he's been dead ten years?'

'Someone interested in 'im? How can that be even possible, Paul?'

'Billy, I don't have a clue, which is why I'm asking, and between us we have to make a start on finding out the answer. So tell me about the main men and their relationship with Field and then I'll leave you in peace to get on with your life. OK?'

'Roger that, mate. Peace? Probably not possible with an 'ardcase like you.'

Paul ignored the inference. 'Come on, Billy, talk to me.'

'Well I suppose the main men were Bruce Reynolds, Ronald Buster Edwards, Charlie Wilson and Gordon Goody. Reynolds was the leader, Wilson the paymaster, the man who counted up the cash and divvied it out afterwards, Buster and Gordon Goody were lieutenants to Bruce Reynolds. If I was a guessin' man, Paul, I'd say it would be these four who were once and might still be interested in Field. But in truth, mate, I can't really see it now.'

'Why so, Billy?'

'Well, I'll explain it to yer. Might 'elp, like.'

'Go on.'

'Except for old Bruce, the other three were sort o' connected to Field in a number of ways before the actual robbery job. Buster and Gordon Goody were crooks from way back and Brian Field used to give 'em inside knowledge for 'ouse robberies. 'E was some sort of lawyers clerk and picked up the info from 'is firm's clients, like, and passed it on to the boys. 'E also fitted up some legal help for the two o' them on more than one occasion. Buster got done on a stolen car charge and Brian fixed the defence.'

'So, Field was a pretty useful man, then, Billy. What else was there? What happened on the Robbery?'

'Well, Bruce Reynolds and the other three used to run around as the main players in the South West Gang, leastways that was what the bleedin' Flying Squad called 'em.'

'Was Field a member?' Paul asked.

'No, but he got mixed up with 'em after they done the Airport Job at 'Eathrow. Goody and Charlie Wilson got lifted and Brian managed to 'elp 'em both get bail.'

'So where's Field's link to the Train Robbery?' Paul was getting impatient. He wanted Hopkins to get to the point - if there was one. He had to make a connection between a long-dead man and Victoria Walker-Haig; and so far there was none that he could see.

'I only know what I 'eard, Paul, and it's fuckin' old news now, remember, like I said.'

'Just tell it, Billy.'

'Well the talk was that the South West Gang, Reynolds to be more precise, wanted to do somethin' really big, somethin' that Bruce considered would set 'em all up for life.' Hopkins paused and a rueful expression crossed his face. 'An' I suppose that's exactly what 'e did, in a way, somethin' totally fuckin' life-changin'. What a laugh, eh.'

'Billy,' Paul coaxed him.

'Yeh. So it was Brian Field who brought in the Ulsterman, as the bloke was called. 'E 'ad the inside info about the Royal Mail train running from Glasgow to Euston and stopping to pick up all the old banknotes on the way. Field acted as the go between. An' 'cause 'e worked in a lawyers office', Bruce used 'im to arrange the purchase of the farm they all went to after the robbery. But that was a bollocks as it turned out.'

'How so?'

'Because Field was supposed to supervise the cleanout of the farm so as not to leave any forensics, but 'e didn't do it properly. Also, after Charlie Wilson 'ad counted all the cash and Reynolds 'ad said what the share-outs and the one-off payments was to be, Field was supposed to pass the monies on to the others that was to be paid. There was a bloke called Mark in all this, an' Field's wife.'

'His wife?' Paul interjected. Was this it, he wondered? It was the first piece of information that Hopkins had mentioned that leaped out of his narrative. 'What was her name?'

'She was called Karin.' Karin and not Sian. Paul sniffed something vital here amongst the junkyard of Billy Hopkins information and the story Victoria had told. And was it a German name? Hopkins went on. 'Field got 'is one-seventeenth and was trusted by Reynolds and Wilson to get the share to the Ulsterman and to give the pay-off to Mark, the bloke what was goin' to do the forensic clean of the farm. 'E was a van driver as well. And after they all left the farm, they drove in two vans back to Brian Field's place in Oxfordshire somewhere. Karin drove the other van. Buster always said that Field's wife Karin should 'ave been on the job instead of 'er 'usband. Said she was cool as a cucumber, throughout.'

'Go on.'

'Only problem was the cleanup was a bollocks, like I said, and when the Flying Squad found the place there was forensics all over it. That's 'ow the boys got nabbed. So they all bailed the gaff and went their own different ways, with various results as I expect you know or 'ave read about, Major.' Billy Hopkins looked seriously at Paul. 'As I said, Paul, a fuckin' long time ago now. So what's this really all about then?'

'Brian Field, Billy, that's what this is all about. So the reason why any of the Robbers would have been after Field would have been because of the money?'

'Guess so, Paul. But 'ere's the thing, and the reason why it don't ring true to me. They're all old, fucked or overseas now. Field's been dead ten years and for ten years before that 'e was livin' under a false name and apart from anythin' else,' and Hopkins looked knowingly at Paul, ''is money was recovered, well a lot of it was.' Hopkins laughed gently at his own black humour.

'What do you mean?'

'Bruce Reynolds got out in seventy-eight, went back in again in eighty but now is broke, livin' on income support and 'as been since the last eight or nine years. 'E's down in Croydon, I think, and 'is son, Nick, is a musician. 'E's more interested in selling 'is story than anythin' else.'

Was it Field's money? Paul asked himself. He wasn't yet sure he was getting anywhere. He looked at his watch. It was four o'clock. He wanted to be on the road in the next ten minutes but he still needed something more tangible to justify his planned trip down to Portland.

'What about the others, Billy?'

'Well for a start Buster's selling flowers at Waterloo station as I told you earlier. 'E's got no money but also no real appetite for the criminal life anymore. Does a bit of fraud and gentle stuff every now and then but I wouldn't be surprised if the poor bloke didn't top 'imself sometime. 'E's a depressing man to be with. Only got a brother.' So unlikely to be Reynolds or Edwards, Paul thought, nor their families. Hopkins said, 'Gordon Goody's in Spain and went there since 'is release in seventy-five. Then there's Charlie Wilson and what a fucker 'e is! Dangerous man, Paul, and if anyone was likely to get arsey about bein' cheated of money by Brian Field then it might be Charlie Wilson. But again, Major, I don't reckon so.'

'Why not, Billy?'

'When 'e was released in seventy-eight, Field 'ad already disappeared, so to speak, 'adn't 'e? And Charlie went to Spain. 'E's still there and into all sorts of nonsense, I've 'eard, drug smuggling and gun running, the lot. Wouldn't be surprise if 'e didn't cop it sometime very soon. Down in Marbella. What a shit-'ole that is.'

So the watchers or searchers weren't one of the four Billy Hopkins had talked about, if what he said was correct. Paul was as sure as he could be of this. There was too much

167

elapsed time, too many other factors that had woven themselves into these four men's lives, and Brian Field had been off their own individual radars for too long when the four of them were finally released from prison. If any of them had wanted to find Field, then it would have been in the period from seventy-five onwards. By then, according to Victoria, Brian Field was Brian Carlton, probably had been since soon after his release in nineteen sixty-seven, *eight years earlier than Edwards and Goody and eleven years earlier than Reynolds and Wilson.*

'Field's money, Billy, what happened to it? You said a lot of it had been recovered. How?'

'Seems no one rightly knows, Paul. What was found was found was in a bag in Dorking Woods. Discovered by some walkers after 'is arrest. But accordin' to the press the money found would 'ave been about two-thirds of Field's actual share, one-seventeenth of the total haul, which was about one 'undred and fifty thousand in old money. A fuckin' fortune by today's values though.'

'So why would anyone be interested in Field's money if it had largely gone.' Paul asked this mainly of himself, thinking out loud.

Billy Hopkins answered for him. ''Cause it was reckoned Field 'ad scarpered with the Ulsterman's share and the payout for the van driver. That's why, in my 'umble view.'

Bingo! It *was* money and it always had to have been. Nothing else made sense. And if, as Hopkins said, Field made off with the Ulsterman's share and the money for the clean-up man, Mark, then with what he had left from his own share there was a pretty sizeable pot of gold. Which was why Brian Field had very quickly changed his identity, why he always had money when Victoria Walker-Haig knew him as Brian Carlton, and why he was worried about security to the extent that he had asked his new wife Sian to put a small attaché case into safekeeping in the bank...the weekend before he was killed and all his secrets died with him.

'You could be right, Billy,' Paul said.

'Fuckin' right I am, Major Stanton. Well worth lookin' for at least,' responded Billy Hopkins.

But would it have been the other Great Train Robbers? Yes, probably, in the immediate aftermath of the Robbery, whilst they were still on the loose. But possibly not after they had been released from prison, because by then Field was Carlton and had almost totally disappeared into a new life. Or had he? Who knew about him or who would go to some lengths to try and find out? Someone, or else why had Field been paranoid about security in those weeks before he was killed?

Paul had another thought. The first wife. 'Tell me about his wife, Karin?' Paul asked. This had to be it, the link he was looking for.

'She was a German bint. Divorced Brian when 'e was in prison. Married another German. Some kind of journalist, I think. Started writin' all sorts of tosh about the robbery after it 'appened and the main men were on the run, abroad or already banged up inside. As I told you, Paul, she was up for it, apparently. A right tough woman from what I 'eard, but a lovely looker, too.'

German! There it was! And Brian Field's first wife would definitely want his money if for no other reason than she had been involved and been cheated of any reward. So had she watched and waited all these years to find her late-ex-husband's money? And was she still there, in or close to Portland in some way, having established Victoria as the only possible link to Field's past? Well he'd find out. And then Hopkins said something that Paul instantly realised was very significant.

'But thinkin' about all that old money, Paul, it was all ones and fivers, nineteen sixty-three banknotes. The value of it today would be fantastic, but,' and Billy Hopkins nodded knowingly at Paul as he said this, 'no one could trade those notes in for anythin'.' And he was right. Brian Carlton couldn't possibly have been spending Great Train Robbery banknotes ten years ago when he was living the high life and travelling around Europe with the Children's Book Centre. So what had he been spending and what had he left behind in assets that made Victoria Walker-Haig a target, even today?

'Thanks a lot, Billy, you've been a great help. Please tell no one about this conversation. It never happened. Get my drift?'

'Sort of, Major. Mum's the word, eh.'

'It is. If you go blabbing your mouth off, Billy, you might end up being visited by the Boys from the Boathouse.'

'What? What boys are those, Major?'

'You don't want to know, Billy.'

Paul Stanton got up and left. He was on his way to Portland.

16

TO PORTLAND

PAUL STOPPED AT the Fleet Services and made a 'phone call. The telephone was answered quickly and Paul asked for someone and waited a minute. It was five-thirty in the afternoon and still a little early, but he was in luck.

'Hello, Barry Radford. Who's this?'

'Barry, it's Paul Stanton.'

'Paul! Good to hear from you. Where are you?'

'Fleet Services, on my way down to your neck of the woods, Portland.'

'Now what sort of business might it be that brings you down to Portland? You know there's water in this part of the world and it doesn't suit land grunts such as you!' It was a poor attempt at humour but Paul smiled inwardly. 'I thought you were bottled up in the MoD, Paul,' Radford continued. 'Oh, and congrats on the promotion, by the way, we all thought it was well deserved. So you're officially going to be one of those high-flyers now!' The man on the end of the call laughed out loud. 'But you do realise don't you, my old Army mate, that a lieutenant colonel in the Army only equates to a major in the Royal Marines!'

'I know, I know, and you're a major in the Marines, so I'll never aspire to the lofty heights of you and your fellow bootnecks,' Paul responded, using one of the numerous slang terms for the Royal Marines. 'And you're the Senior Service, etc, etc, all of which I agree with without any resistance, but I need your help, Barry.'

'Go for it, my friend, what can I do for you?'

'Any chance you can skive off for a couple of days and come down to Portland with me? I need some eyes and some muscle and someone I can trust.' Paul hoped Barry Radford wouldn't um and ah about his request. The two of them had history together in both troubled and peaceful times and were close friends. Radford's response didn't disappoint Paul's expectations.

'Hmm, it's a bit of an ask but I might be able to. Let me think...we're in the middle of a training week so I could easily spin some yarn about a recce in Portland or something equally unbelievable as far as the CO is concerned. I could probably bail out from here at lunchtime or even late morning tomorrow and be with you shortly after. Any good?'

'Perfect. Thanks, Barry. Come with only civvy kit. We'll need stealth gear. Probably some basic grade munitions. It's low-key but might escalate. It's also deniable, untraceable and non-military.'

'For Christ's sake, Paul, what the hell have you got yourself into this time?'

'Nothing the two of us can't handle but I won't tell you about it on the 'phone right now. Come to a place called the Cove Inn when you arrive tomorrow. Know it?'

172

'I do. Can't wait to drink in it again.'

'Good. I'll be there unless something unforeseen happens, and if it does I'll leave a message for you at the bar. Oh, and tomorrow, as you're leaving, can you just go via the town library and do some quick research on a bloke called Brian Field. He was a Great Train Robber.'

'He was a what? A Great Train Robber! Have you lost the plot, Stanton, that was twenty-five years ago, wasn't it? OK. I'll do it but I'm not that happy, mate. I gave up research work ages ago.'

Paul ignored Radford's gentle moan. 'I need you to try and dig out some old newspaper cuttings from the time during his trial and after his imprisonment and note any references to his wife. It was nineteen sixty-three through to sixty-seven or something like that. The wife was a German woman called Karin. It shouldn't take you that long to put it all together. Ring them now if they're still open or in the morning first thing, and ask them to get the stuff ready. The material's likely to be on microfiche. If you can't do it tomorrow, Barry, then it'll be a real pain and I don't think we have the time to do it in Portland or Weymouth.'

'Fucking hell, Paul, sounds serious stuff. Should I talk to my Dad about this woman?' It sounded improbable but Barry Radford was asking a serious question.

'No, not yet at any rate. We might need him later, but only as a last resort.'

'So for the moment we're on our own?'

'We are. There's a bed for you but bring some lightweight outdoor gear for both of us just in case, as well as the other stuff.'

'Wilco, boss. Sounds like we might need some appropriate wheels as well as stowage and storage space so I'll come in the old jalopy, the Rover, you remember her?' Paul grunted. He did. Radford was referring to his beaten up long wheelbase Land Rover, bashed, dented and paint scarred, but it went like a dream and had four-wheel drive. Paul knew it to be uncomfortable but it would be perfect.

'Perfect, Barry. See you tomorrow.'

* * *

PAUL ATE THE crisps he'd bought, drove and thought about things. He had another two hours to go at least, but he knew the route as far as Dorchester and could do it on autopilot.

Yes, Barry Radford was the man to share this mission and Paul was relieved he was in the UK. Radford was with the Special Boat Service, the SBS, in Poole, which was no more than an hour's drive away from Portland along the coast road. Currently he was commanding C Squadron, the swimmer and canoe operations sub unit, and from what he'd said he and his men were on refresher and qualification training in their base in Hamworthy.

Paul kept in touch with all the friends who, like him, had a part of their lives shrouded in the black world of the UK's elite Special Forces. He and Barry Radford had first met in 1981 during Paul's third tour in Northern Ireland as the

Officer Commanding the SAS Troop, based in the Hanger in RAF Aldergrove. Although a Royal Marine, Barry Radford had passed SAS Selection and his specialist qualifications for the SBS and volunteered for Northern Ireland. He was Paul's second-in-command. Their friendship had started from that time and developed afterwards when Barry had been the Adjutant of 21 SAS, the famous Artists' Rifles, in 1984, working and living in London at the time when Paul was escaping from the Staff College course and living whenever he could in Lupus Street. They were both members of the Special Forces Club. They were both hard working and dedicated…to their men, careers and life. Say no more.

Paul had enjoyed those few good times together before he had finished the Staff Course, left his home in London and returned to regimental duty. Before Crossmaglen and the subsequent horrors of his covert and deadly mission in Ireland and Germany. He shuddered slightly at the memories, as if someone had walked over his grave; which in a way they had because he could scent uncertainty in the course of action he and Barry Radford were about to embark on, and perversely there was a *German connection* of some sort.

Yes, there was risk out there but he didn't have a measure of it. And this was England. He was not sanctioned by HMG to seek out and deliver retribution as he had been in Ireland and Berlin. Nor was it Nepal, where, with the caution they had exercised and the support of his Gurkhas, they'd been able to deal with the Hungarian thugs in the only manner such people understood. They'd got away with mayhem and killing. He and Radford couldn't go down that route in England.

Paul concentrated on the driving and took stock. He was making good progress. He'd come off the M3 Motorway some time ago and was now in the tortuous process of winding his way around Ringwood. With luck he'd be on the outskirts of Dorchester in an hour, maybe less, and then he'd have to resort to the map Victoria had given him of how to find her cottage.

He'd memorised the main routes and Nikki had run him through them again before he left. South from Dorchester, over the Ridgeway towards Weymouth Bay, down to the beachfront and the Jubilee Clock, turn right up onto Westwey, alongside the Harbour, up out of the town and then turn down towards the Ferry Bridge with Chesil Beach on your right side and HMS Osprey and Portland Harbour on your left, until you hit the Royal Manor of Portland itself. Victoria's cottage was close to Chesil and up into the little village area called Chiswell. It was a one-minute walk from the Cove Inn, he'd been told.

The thing that concerned Paul most was that the two men who had stalked and frightened Victoria might not be in Portland anymore. If they'd left the area it would be impossible for him to track them. They had last seen her on Saturday night. They'd found her home and seen her inside it, so would they have thought it odd for her to disappear from her cottage for all of yesterday and today? Would they think she'd just gone to visit family and friends for an overnight but would be back soon, and so wait in the area longer?

Paul didn't really have a clue as to the answer. But worrying would do no good. He'd find out soon enough. If what he thought was correct, the men were mere foot soldiers and so far they were still empty-handed. Whoever was their boss would want results. Yes, he thought, they'd still be there and he was almost with them.

Paul drove slowly through the summer evening traffic towards Ferry Bridge and the panorama of Chesil Beach, Portland Harbour, the Naval Base and the steep craggy features of Portland. It was a magnificent view. He thought of Nikki and his heart clenched with a tightness of deep, deep affection. He would call her later. This was her home territory. He wondered when and if the two of them would be able to walk through this wonderful part of England's coast and let the romance and beauty of it feed the love in their souls. He had no idea, if he was honest with himself. Nikki was due to fly back to Kathmandu at the weekend. Focus, Stanton, good things lay ahead, of that he was sure, but first there was the mystery of The Great Train Robber to unravel.

Barry Radford had asked Paul if he should contact his father to see if he could find out anything about Brian Field's first wife. Coincidentally, Barry's father was a senior detective in the Metropolitan Police and had worked in the London area all his life, so he *would* be able to help, if asked, Paul believed. But it was too soon. There were too many uncertainties about the whole situation and Paul needed much more detail before he asked for official help. If there was danger and dirty business ahead then he and Radford had the skills to deal with it. Paul hated the idea of a vulnerable woman being stalked and terrorised by criminals over stolen money, so he would find out what was going on and eliminate the threat.

He found the cottage and parked three doors up from it on the opposite side of the road. The place was a labyrinth of narrow streets with off shoots of even narrower alleys all leading up into the area called Fortuneswell or onto Chesil. The cottages were terraced, built of weathered and dull looking stone, hugger-mugger. It was almost eight-thirty and he was pleased with the timings. It was still daylight but the sun was dipping. As Nikki had said, it promised to be a spectacular sunset over the area where he supposed the Cove Inn was. There were few people around now; most would be in the pubs or back in their holiday accommodation after an enjoyable tiring day by the seaside.

Paul sat and observed the area for a couple of minutes. There was absolutely no movement, nor was there light on in any of the houses. Victoria's was as she had described it: next to a garage, which she had access to from inside, with a front aspect bay window. There was a narrow alleyway on the other side that led to the back of her cottage. It seemed very private.

Paul unlocked the front door, stepped quickly inside and shut the door behind him. He stood and listened. All was still and quiet. There was no movement. A car drove down the road and its noise quickly disappeared. There was sufficient ambient light for him to see.

Something was wrong. Paul could sense it.

He walked into the narrow hallway, moving cautiously. Victoria had described the layout and he knew the living rooms were off to the right with the stairs dead ahead that led to the upper rooms. Beyond the stairs towards the back of the cottage was the open plan kitchen from which Victoria accessed her studio and the adjacent garage. The kitchen had a back door that led to the small Mediterranean garden, the garden from where the Germans had looked in on her on Saturday night.

All the doors were wide open and as he looked inside Paul's face tightened and he felt his anger rise. It was obvious the place had been lovingly created and furnished, but every single room had been searched and comprehensively pulled apart. He moved upstairs, knowing what he would find. Victoria's cottage had been trashed. He stood on the landing and listened once again, just to make sure, but there was no one else there. He was furious. The bastards had gone but he would find them and make them pay for what they'd done. But had the Germans found anything? He didn't think so. Victoria's home had been desecrated but Paul could tell it had been a semi-professional search and not thorough enough, in his view, to have found the long-lost attaché case, particularly as it was unlikely the men knew exactly what they were looking for.

Assuming of course that the attaché case was actually somewhere in the house.

Paul went downstairs and switched on all the lights. He wanted the watchers to know the cottage was still occupied. He checked the telephone line and heard the gentle purring of the dial tone. He was thinking furiously about how to play his next steps, but his first job was to call Nikki. Which he did.

Something had been nagging at him all the way down to Portland. Something connected to the money. There was information he needed and only she could find it. He told her about it.

Afterwards, Paul pulled a pair of worn Levis from his bag and changed his boat shoes for some desert boots. He needed to be dressed for the part. He left some background light on in the cottage, locked up as he left and went to the pub in search of some German housebreakers.

17

THE GERMANS

PAUL FOUND THEM in the Cove Inn and was grateful his luck seemed to be in. At least he hoped it was.

They were sitting at a beer-stained wooden trestle table just to the left of the entrance door with their backs to the small bay window that gave the view out over the sea. The sun was now dipping spectacularly onto the horizon. The ocean's flat expanse was a panorama of stillness, broken only by the dappling gentle wake of the lobster boats coming home from the day's fishing, having re-baited their pots.

The late evening sky was flooded with broken streaks of weak blood-red lines, mixed crazily with the darkening of the failing day and the reflected purple and magenta from the sky that bounced off the calm of the deep blue sea. It was magnificent and it was what all the drinkers were looking at as they thronged the sea wall outside the pub. It was what all those inside the pub were looking at through the various windows in the two other small snug rooms to the left and right of the bar area where Paul now stood.

'Good evening,' Paul said to the woman behind the copper-topped bar, who smiled and enquired what he wanted to drink with a raising of her eyebrows.

'Hello, sir, what will you have?' She was the only one serving.

'Are you by any chance the landlady?' Was this the woman who had tipped off Victoria Walker-Haig a few days ago?

'I am!'

It was quiet time. Everyone had a drink and was watching the sunset and talking quietly. Everyone, that was, except for the two men dressed in hot-looking shirts and sleeveless sweaters, who wore frowns of concern on their unshaven faces and were not remotely interested in the natural beauty of this English coast phenomenon.

Paul put his tactic into operation. 'A pint of lager, please.' As the woman started to draw his pint, Paul half-turned towards the door entrance and the table area where the two men sat and said, 'I'm a close friend of Vikki Walker-Haig. I understand this is her local when she's in Portland. In fact I'm staying at her cottage. She very kindly gave me her keys.' He turned back to the bar. 'I'll be here for a couple of days,' and Paul pulled out the house keys from his jeans' pocket and showed them to the landlady, smiling his biggest and most winning smile as he did so.

The woman's manner warmed immediately as she gave him his drink. 'Well if that's so, sir, we'll look forward to seeing you in here again, won't we? Just like Vikki. She's gone away has she?'

'She has, for a long while this time,' and Paul sipped his lager. 'Delicious, thank you. Just what's needed after a hot one like today.' He turned around again and noticed the interest with which the two men had picked up on this piece of social conversation and were now staring intently at him. He looked at them directly and dipped his head as if to say good evening. There was an edge of unease in their demeanour. 'Fantastic sunset,' he opined. The two men said nothing.

'It always is,' said the landlady, and Paul turned back to her. Another couple came in through the door and up to the bar and there was a slight shuffling of movement at the table by the window. There was just something out of place about the men and he was sure they were the two he was looking for. His instincts were telling him so and they'd seldom been wrong in the past. Paul decided this was the moment to put his play into action. He would chance it.

'Maybe you can help me,' he said to the landlady as she was starting to serve the other couple. 'Vikki told me she thought there might be some people looking for her but they never made contact. But that would be a bit odd, wouldn't it? Do you know of anyone who was looking for her?' He paused and smiled beguilingly at the woman. The landlady did nothing more than open her eyes wide, look beyond Paul and nod her head fractionally.

'Thanks,' he said.

Great! He thought. Got it! Don't involve the landlady, Stanton. Keep it strictly personal.

Paul walked from the bar towards the two men at their table with his pint of lager in his right hand and his eyes focused on the splendid scene being performed by Nature outside the window. He couldn't tell the size of the men accurately but the one on his right was of smallish build, with dark slicked-back hair and furtive eyes set too close together. He was weasely and wiry and looked to be no threat. The second man on Paul's left was bigger, with broad shoulders, close cropped hair and a swarthy countenance. He looked a little like Desperate Dan and Paul hoped he had the mental acuity of the comic character and not the physical ability. But no matter, he'd take care of it. He noticed the two of them were wearing summer shoes. Their legs and feet were clearly visible underneath the trestle bar table. Good.

Paul stopped a pace short of the table and leaned forwards as if to peer through the window at the sunset. He was aware of the men shifting and looking at him. He ignored them and moved decisively forwards. His right foot shot out under the table and trampled the ankle of the man on his right. It was a vicious move and Paul put all his weight into the stomping action. The man lurched backwards. '*Du Mistkerl,*' he swore, his voice rising as the pain hit him. '*Du Kannst gleich eine haben,*' he said as he then recoiled forwards and bent his head and went to pull his damaged leg inwards. Paul fell towards them as if stumbling and threw the contents of his pint glass over the two men, rocking the table forwards with his thighs and pinning them into their bench.

The second man was in motion. '*Verdammtes Schwein...*' he started to say, so Paul turned as if towards the first man and in doing so swung his left elbow round in a smashing blow to the right side of the man's neck. That's for swearing in public, he thought, even if it was in German and he didn't fully understand it.

It was uproar. The German expletives were coming thick and fast from the first man. The second man was blinking from pain and the lager in his eyes and struggling to keep consciousness.

'Goodness, what a mess, what can I say?' Paul stepped back from the shambles of wounded bodies, disrupted furniture, spilt drink and social disturbance he had created. 'And you're visitors, as well. How terrible of me. So you're German? *Ich spreche ein bisschen Deutsch,*' he announced to them proudly.

'Let me help you.' The landlady had come round to him, as had the couple that was being served, just to observe, probably.

'I'm sure it's fine,' Paul said, turning to the woman. 'A cloth to wipe up the mess would be most useful.' Paul studied the two Germans with the best look of faked innocence he could muster. 'Are you both OK?'

'No. *Scheisse,*' said the first man. 'We are not.' His English was heavily accented. He looked up at Paul and his eyes burned in anger. But he was limp wristed and feeble despite his outrage, Paul could see it in his posture and pathetic defiance. The other man was still coming to terms with his dislocated mind and was also no threat. They were low-grade watchers and reporters, Paul decided, brains and brawn, but low-grade nonetheless. There was someone or some persons far more significant behind these two wretched specimens of humanity. He'd find them in due course; but meanwhile there

185

was still another act to put into the particular stage play he had created, and he needed to be a touch cautious.

'Look, I'm terribly sorry,' he said looking suitably chastised and apologetic. The landlady was cleaning up the table with a large cloth. The two other people had wandered off - disturbance and excitement over, it seemed - and the pub was returning to its prior state of grace. The sun was sinking gloriously into the sea, nothing was really amiss, it all said. 'Can I at least invite you both back to the cottage I'm staying in for some supper. To make amends for my clumsiness?' Paul implored. 'You may know the place. It's just up the road from here, only a minute away,' he said, thinking he'd just throw this piece of temptation their way to see if it elicited any signals.

'No, *nein*, thank you,' replied the first man. 'We must go back now.' He looked shifty as he said this, as if he was hiding some guilty secret. They know the cottage, Paul decided, and they know I'm not the person they were supposed to find there. The game has changed so it depends on whether or not they can cope with the changes.

'Well hopefully I'll see you both again and can make some compensation to you.'

'Yes, *danke*, perhaps. We are staying a few days more.'

Fantastic! Paul's gambit was definitely in play. He moved back to the bar as the Germans struggled out of the door clutching the remnants of their composure. They looked a sorry pair: both dripping wet, with one hobbling on a badly damaged ankle and the other clutching his head and his friend's shoulder. He waved a casual goodbye as the door closed.

'Sorry about all that,' he said to the landlady who was back behind the bar. 'May I ask your name and can I please have a replacement pint!'

She laughed out loud. 'I'm Emily and did you do that on purpose?'

'What on earth makes you think so?' Paul responded jauntily as he drank thirstily from his recharged glass.

'Because I have the feeling you did and it's the way you reacted,' she replied. 'I also have the feeling you're quite a bad and mischievous man.'

'Well, Emily, you may well be right, but I need to ask you a question.'

She looked at him earnestly. 'Who are you, anyway?'

'I'm a friend, Emily, a friend, that I promise.'

'Well in that case go ahead, mister, ask your question.'

'Any idea where those two men are staying? It would be in Vikki's interest that I knew. If you happen to know, that is.'

'Very mysterious, you are, friend. They're in the Pennsylvania Castle. It's a big hotel up on the way to Southwell and the Bill. I've heard them speaking about it.' Emily paused and frowned before she spoke again. 'They're creepy,' she said seriously, 'and they've been coming around here for the last few days and asking questions about Vikki and whatnot. We've not liked it nor said anything. We Portland folk are close and take care of each other. And there's someone else up there in the Castle, I'm sure of it from what they've been saying. We hear things from behind the bar and they don't speak quiet those two with their bloody foreign language. Where's Vikki gone? Is she all right?'

Paul drank down his lager. 'Yes, Emily, Vikki is very well and very safe. Thanks for the drink and you've been a fantastic help. I'm off to the chip shop. All that excitement has made me hungry.' Paul smiled at her.

'Come in tomorrow, then, friend.'

'I might. But I'm spoken for, mind!' laughed Paul as he left.

He looked for the Germans as he walked down the stone-strewn alleyway from the Cove Inn to the street, but there was no sign of them. They would have had a car if they were going back to the Pennsylvania Castle. Tomorrow Barry Radford would be with him and that was exactly what Paul needed: mutual support, fresh eyes, another viewpoint and a best friend who was not averse to a little mayhem and violence if necessary, which he believed would be the case.

It was only ten o'clock and was just about dark. He was satisfied with the way things had gone but he was also famished, and he had a lot of clearing up and searching to do before his night was over.

Paul Stanton walked the few yards down the street to a place where he bought some of Portland's famous fish and chips, which he ate on the move on his way back to the wreckage of Victoria's home.

18

FOLLOW THE MONEY

PAUL RANG NIKKI again just before ten o'clock in the morning. He'd got up early, finished off putting the cottage to rights and had coffee and toast before he made the call. He hoped she'd had some time to find out what he'd asked her about last night.

'I'm worried about you, Paul,' Nikki replied after he'd quickly given her an update. The concern was evident in her voice and it made him feel very good. 'I spoke to Vikki last night and had to tell her what had happened. She was relatively philosophical about it and I told her you'd sort everything out. She's already on her way to Heathrow and is well out of harm's way.'

'She is, and I'm going to be fine, Nik, and the cottage looks OK after a bit of the Stanton organisational tender loving care. Not too much damage once I'd straightened everything out.'

'What will you do, Paul?'

'I have more searching to do. Your sister has a ton of old packing cases in the garage and of course there's the attic, which I'm looking forward to. But my reinforcement is

189

arriving early afternoon and then we'll be a match for anyone or anything and you never know what the two of us might be able to find. I'm hopeful. Always optimistic.'

'Who is it, Paul?'

'An old mate of mine called Barry Radford. You'll meet him soon, I hope, and you'll love him, especially as he's a bit of hunk, although he does have a pretty steady partner, a South African girl. Anyway, he's in the SBS, so much like me he's used to danger and mayhem and more than capable of taking care of things, and me for that matter.'

'You silly man,' she chided him gently. 'You know I'm spoken for and simply do not have eyes for anyone else!'

'Funny you should say that. I had to say the same thing to the landlady in the Cove last night.'

'Paul!'

'Seriously, though, Nikki, listen to me, please. You don't need to know too much. You understand why, don't you?'

'I do.'

'And you must concentrate on your meetings with MozLon on Thursday and not worry about things down here. You know how vital it is for Danny's Gurkha business to get the Mozambique contract, and it's important for you, too.'

'You're right, and I will concentrate, but everything's changing, Paul.' He let the conversation hang there for a second. They both knew Nikki had to return to Kathmandu at the end of the week and that if Danny Dalloway's company, Gurkha Connections Limited, won the security contract from MozLon, then the future would become dramatically uncertain and the two of them would be separated by vast distance and different priorities. But they'd agreed they would deal with the impact of this on their newfound relationship one step at a time, just as Paul had to deal with the Germans now, one step at a time.

He changed the subject. 'What we talked about last night, did you manage to find out anything? I know it's still early, but did you?'

'I did! Well a little bit.' Paul could hear the excitement she felt in her voice. 'I spoke to a friend in the finance sector and he asked me to hang on while he did some checking. Well, when he came back on the 'phone he said that by his colleagues' calculations, using the inflation figures they had to hand, a sum of money totalling two hundred and ten thousand pounds in nineteen sixty-three would be equivalent to approximately one million pounds in nineteen seventy-nine! How amazing is that!'

'Amazing,' responded Paul thoughtfully. He had calculated the various sums of Train Robbery money Brian Field had been paid and allegedly made off with from the information Billy Hopkins had given him. Two hundred and ten thousands pounds, which didn't include the money found in Dorking Woods. Now it was beginning to make proper sense to him. 'And in today's money terms?' Paul asked.

'Double!' Nikki said excitedly.

And of course, during the period when he ran southern Europe's operations for the Children's Book Centre and cash was king and whilst Victoria Walker-Haig was working for him some of the time, who could say whether Brian Carlton

191

would have been adding to this stash of money with selective cash injections from some of the book exhibitions he ran in Europe's capital cities? Smart man, the bastard, thought Paul. Once a crook always a crook. And because Brian Carlton would not have been able to do anything with a mass of five and one pound notes from the Great Train Robbery, he'd have had to launder them somehow and turn them into *saleable assets*.

'Did you manage to ask your expert about investment options?' Paul asked.

'I did, my Paul, and he said in his opinion, and stressed it was only his opinion, the best investments throughout that time and still today, by the way, if you've got any spare cash, Mr Soldier, would have been and are gold and diamonds. How about that!'

Bingo! 'Nicola Double Scotch, you are amazing,' he said. 'I would like to talk to you for the rest of my life, but now I have to go and find the enemy again.'

'You do, Stanton, and besides I have work to do, too.'

'I'll call tonight but I don't know what time it will be.'

'I'll be here, Paul, in your lovely home, and you can call at any time of day and night. Just call. OK?'

'I will.'

Paul hung up and stood and thought for a moment. He checked his watch - just after ten o'clock. Whilst he'd been talking to Nikki he'd been watching through the bay window in the lounge and the street outside was busy but not unusually so. There had been no sign of the Germans.

He was now almost certain what was in the attaché case. And he was almost certain he knew what Brian Field-Carlton had done and why the Germans were after the case. The talk of the money had fired his blood again and he decided he was damned well going to find it! Victoria Walker-Haig had said she believed the attaché case must still be in her possession and so, he reasoned, it was in the cottage somewhere, hidden deep, buried in the accumulated detritus and junk of her life over the ensuing years. The Germans hadn't found it, but he would.

It would be somewhere unlikely. Victoria would have noticed it, otherwise. He'd start with the storage areas, including loft accesses and the adjoining garage, and tick them off one-by-one. He would leave the main rooms to the last because the Germans had searched them and found nothing and nor had he when he'd restored them to their former state of tidiness.

Paul Stanton went to work. He had three hours before he expected Barry Radford could get to Portland, and when he did the two of them would go and find the Germans again.

But before that he needed to have results. He needed to find the money.

* * *

PAUL WAS OUTSIDE the Cove Inn looking over the flat calm of the sea, appreciating the strong heat of another hot July day and sipping a pint of shandy. All the pub's customers were doing the same, thronging the terrace and looking at the other people, the ocean and the pebbled features of Chesil Beach. It was busy yet quiet and reflective at the same time, no one was talking much, just looking. Children were scampering around on the pebbles below the terrace and playing dare with the waves on the very edge of the sea. All the noise was in front of him and away to his left, along the stretch of the beach towards the craggy headland of Portland.

Paul's thoughts were all over the place as a result of his morning's activity and he was constantly reviewing options and implications. So far, though, the Germans were nowhere to be seen and it was now well into lunchtime. Then, as if to help focus his quixotic mind, the noiselessness was broken by the distinctive gurgle of a vehicle coming into the small parking area down below behind him and he recognized the sound of an old Land Rover. It had to be Barry Radford's.

He turned around and walked a couple of paces away from everyone and saw the battered hulk of the vehicle, with its moldy canopy strapped down tightly. He couldn't resist a smile as it pulled into a space. Now the action can really start, he thought. But we need to find those Germans.

Radford climbed out of the driver's door and stood and stretched, scanning the area. He looked fit and tanned and was wearing faded blue Levi's, a much-washed olive green polo shirt and desert boots. Paul watched him for a few seconds before calling out his greeting. He liked this man very much and his mere presence suddenly infused Paul with a sense of invincibility.

'Hello you battered, ugly bootneck bastard!' Paul moved down the weathered stone steps to the shingled parking area and clapped him on the shoulder. 'How are you?'

'Fuck off, Stanton! You may be smooth but you pongos never did appreciate the Senior Service or its brilliant land component. We Marines taught you bloody infanteers everything you know.'

'Rude and predictable as ever!' said Paul, smiling.

Radford laughed and turned towards Paul. 'I'm fine, mate, thanks, and it's lovely to see this part of the Jurassic Coast once more. Many happy times I've had here amongst the rocks and tides of Portland!'

The two men clasped hands and studied each other briefly. Radford was a bigger man than Paul, but not by much, just broader across the chest and shoulders. They were about the same height, tall, upright men, fit and hard with that look in their eye and the physical demeanour that said to others: "You'd be a fool to tangle with us". They may have been tough, war-seasoned men who understood the responsibility of killing and trying not to be killed by their enemies, but they also had truth, fairness and romance in their souls. They were good men.

Radford's hair was browny-black, thinning around the forehead and cut short everywhere else. His eyes, as he studied Paul, were at first dark and still like bottomless pools, and then the sun bounced off them in kaleidoscopic patterns as he moved his head a nudge and his face brought a smile up from the depths.

'But whether or not it's as lovely to see you again, my old-mate-in-troubled-times,' Radford then said, 'I'll reserve judgment if I may!' And he laughed again and the two men embraced briefly and Paul felt a surge of good feeling flood through him. 'Come on, Stanton, buy a thirsty man a bloody beer, for God's sake! You can afford it now you're about to be a half-colonel!'

'You're on...'

Then the two Germans appeared.

Paul saw them over Radford's shoulder and stopped talking. The two men were walking slowly past the other parked cars, heads bowed and seemingly in deep conversation but coming towards where Paul and Radford stood. All thoughts of a sociable drink and a catch-up on news and gossip went out of the window.

'There they are, Barry, the targets,' Paul said suddenly, turning Radford's body towards the area just to the right of where he'd parked his Land Rover and where the two men were obviously approaching the steps to the Cove Inn.

Radford instantly tuned into the note of seriousness in Paul's voice. 'What, those two? The big ugly crop-headed fucker and the miserable shrivelled bastard with a limp?'

'That's them. I need them in your Rover, bound, immobilized and gagged, and then you and I have to get some info from them. Can you open up the back canopy of your vehicle?'

'Easily. She's ready, rigged and prepped for battle. The big one's mine. Let's move. We can drink beer later.'

And with that Paul Stanton and Barry Radford went into action and the Germans didn't stand a chance.

In practised quickfire movements, Radford loosened the Rover's rear canopy and pulled the pins from the tailboard, dropping it down on its chained restraints. Paul glanced quickly inside and saw the two seatboards on either side had been strapped up and all the gear was neatly stowed in the centre. There seemed to be all sorts of bits and pieces there. Paul trusted Radford implicitly and knew that if he had said it was OK then he had the means to restrain the two Germans. They just had to get the men into the vehicle. Which was going to be no problem. And mercifully, there was no one around in the car park area.

Paul waited those few seconds until the Germans were adjacent to the front of the Land Rover and then stepped forward. Radford was at his shoulder. 'Hello again,' he said, with false lightness in his voice. The two men literally stopped in their tracks and when they looked up their faces were a picture of confusion and surprise, which rapidly turned to alarm as Radford moved forward with obvious mal-intent. Paul said, 'I thought I might have seen you earlier.'

The two Germans were fixed to the spot. Paul and Radford went into action. Radford smashed his elbow into the right side of the big German's head whilst simultaneously kicking the man viciously in the crotch. The man started to crumple like a sack of potatoes being dropped to the ground, but before the German could respond or protest Radford caught him under his arms, stifled his mouth with his left hand and dragged him, shoe heels scraping and bouncing on the rough stones, to the Land Rover and threw him into the back, clambering in himself in almost the same movement.

Simultaneously, with outstretched hand as if to shake that of the other man, Paul grabbed the smaller German's shirt, pulled him violently into his chest, crushed him in a bear-hug of brutal strength, pushed the man's body away from him and smashed his forehead down on the other's with an impact that made the German's eyes cross and instantly glaze with semi-consciousness. Within a matter of seconds all four men were lumbering around in the back of Radford's Land Rover with the tailgate up and pinned in place and the canopy dropped to hide everything from outside view.

It had taken less than thirty seconds to neutralize and take out the two Germans.

'Strap your bastard to the side of the wagon, Paul,' said Radford. 'There are a couple of rigging harnesses by your feet. Strap him up and lash him to the canopy struts. Neutralise the fucker. Straightjacket him. There's duct tape in that basket.' Radford pointed to a metal mesh basket welded onto the front area of the Land Rover just behind the seat backs. 'There are plasticuffs in there as well, so use them.'

'Roger,' responded Paul. He noticed that next to the mesh basket with its loose items was a firmly padlocked metal ammunition box, bolted to the floor of the Land Rover and containing, Paul guessed, munitions - tripflares, smoke grenades and the like - that Radford would have been able to accumulate over the course of time without breaking too many rules and regulations about the accounting and control of such everyday training items. They might need them, he thought, but he hoped not in truth. Mainland UK was a different hunting ground to the wilds of Northern and Southern Ireland, Wall Zone Berlin or Kathmandu. Killing was not an option here. What he needed was non-lethal force to get his answers.

'I'll do the same with this one,' said Radford. 'He's a big bastard, eh.' And with that, as the big German started to wriggle and wrestle, Radford short-punched him under the chin with the flat of his hand and the man went limp. 'But a soft fucker,' said Radford. 'Hardly touched the man; but just as well as I'm guessing we've got some talking to do with these two gentlemen a little later on. Am I right?'

'You are, Barry. And I need to take them some place for a little bit of politically correct interrogation,' replied Paul. 'Know of anywhere hereabouts that might serve us in that line?'

'Of course, Paul, I'm your local guide, remember,' and the two men chuckled, finished their work of trussing, immobilizing and gagging the Germans. They clambered into the front seats of the Rover and Radford took them up into the hinterland of Portland.

They had some information to gather and then they had to follow the money.

Because Paul had done better than the Germans: he'd found the attaché case in Victoria Walker-Haig's cottage; but as yet he had no clue as to who was masterminding the Germans' activities and this he needed to find out as quickly as possible.

* * *

IN THE EVENT it proved easier than Paul had thought. The Germans were not up for self-sacrifice.

'I know just the place,' said Radford. 'We'll bury ourselves in the Withiescroft Quarries, and treat these two gents to a taste of our special hospitality in amongst the majestic landscape of a Portland stone quarry.' He turned to Paul as he drove the Rover up the steep winding road from Fortuneswell towards Easton. 'It's a bleak place and totally private.'

'Sounds perfect,' replied Paul. Now that they had the Germans and he was in Radford's hands as far as the next step was concerned, he'd started to think again about his stunning discovery earlier in the morning. They hadn't even had time to exchange information since Radford arrived, and Paul wondered what his friend had discovered about Brian Field's ex-wife. He decided not to ask just yet. The Germans in the back needed to be deprived of any information. 'How long have we got?' he asked

'It'll take about ten minutes,' said Radford. 'I'm guessing you don't know the layout of the land and the topography. Don't be deceived by the cloak of calm and friendliness of this place in the summer. Portland is one of the ancient promontories of the Jurassic Coast,' said Radford, enjoying his superior knowledge, 'thrusting its famous Bill out into the English Channel and, on days like today, enjoying its balm, but for most of the year absorbing all the battering the mighty Atlantic can inflict upon it.'

Radford changed gears as they approached a roundabout at the top of the climb. 'It has a number of tidal rips as well,' he said. Paul looked back out of the window and the view over Chesil Beach and Portland Harbour towards Weymouth Bay was simply stunning. They headed to Easton. 'Even in these halcyon days of July,' continued Radford, 'we can find a desolate spot. To do so we shall go almost to Easton and then turn off eastwards towards the jagged coast where we will stumble upon the quarries I have in mind.' Radford chuckled. 'How are those two bastards in the back?'

Paul looked behind him. The two Germans hadn't moved. They couldn't. They were trussed to the sidebars of the Land Rover and were totally immobilized. 'They're stewing nicely.'

'Good.'

Paul had found the attaché case inside a large old sports bag stuffed with hockey kit and shin pads. He had started his search in the places he believed the Germans would not have found or had time to explore thoroughly and used a set of rusty ladders to get into the roof area. He'd found the access to this in the very corner of the room Victoria clearly used as a work studio and office. It was hard to get into and even harder to move around in, but sections of it had been clumsily boarded and were stuffed full of the accumulation of her years of college, work and collecting things. There were packing boxes, old cases, mounds and bags of fabrics and clothes, stacks of papers and journals and pieces of surplus furniture crammed into the attic areas. And in amongst this miscellany of her redundant cobwebbed life was the battered sports bag buried amongst some old suitcases, with Brian Field's mildewed attaché case inside it.

Paul had felt a small sense of triumph that he'd found it, that the story was not a fabrication and that there was a good reason for him being here and doing what he'd planned to do with the Germans. But he'd also felt a sense of uncertainty as he'd lifted the bag down and felt its unusual weight - not massively heavy, but a weight of impending trouble - and it struck him with force that inside this innocuous looking piece of hand baggage was a whole heap of problems. He hadn't tried to unlock it since it was closed with two small traditional clasp locks and of course there was no key.

The decision about what to do next had come to him easily because phase one of his mission was accomplished now and he needed to be ready to move into phase two: find the Germans and their mastermind. So he had packed his few things in his grip and stashed this and the attaché case in the boot of his car and tidied the cottage, locking it securely before going to the Cove to meet Barry Radford. He had also decided he would tell no one about what he'd found until he himself knew more and could make a proper decision.

'We're here,' said Radford. 'This'll do, I think.'

Paul had been aware of the changing landscape and the way the Land Rover had started to bump and buck on its suspension as Radford had exited the road and turned into what he assumed was the Withiescroft Quarries. They were moving downwards as well and had driven on for a few more uncomfortable minutes before Radford had let the vehicle come to rest. Paul opened his door and got out to stretch. It was a deserted moonscape of stone blocks and jagged rock edges. They were hidden from view, below the road and the level of the surrounding countryside. Radford had brought them into a minor labyrinth of stone pits and channels. It would do very well, Paul thought.

'Thanks, Barry, let's get these guys out and get to work. Let's hope they talk.' He suddenly felt uncertain about what the Germans might or might not know or say. He had found the money. But where, actually, did it lead? Then Radford's words cut through his mood and fired him up.

'They'll talk, Paul. You have the knack. I know you do.' Radford unpinned the tailgate and dropped it down with a clang. He had the rear canopy up and tied firm and was clambering into the rear space amongst the kit and bodies. 'Come on, you bastards, let's get you unshackled and out in the fresh air. You've got some telling to do,' and with that the smaller German was unceremoniously hauled out of the vehicle and handed to Paul who dumped him on the stony ground. Radford's back emerged as he pulled the larger man over the tailgate and dropped him next to his colleague.

The two Germans sat propped against a large stone; mouths duct-taped and hands zipped firmly with plasticuffs behind their bodies. Their eyes roved the landscape around them and showed confusion and fear. Paul ripped the tape from their mouths and he held a finger to his lips so neither spoke. Besides which, there was nothing to say and no one else was around. They were in a desert of friendless isolation.

'Do you need water?' They nodded their heads. 'Speak to me first, then,' said Paul. 'Tell me who you work for and why you have been following the woman and breaking into her house?' Paul gestured to Radford with a drinking motion and he went back into the Rover to find his water bottles. Paul said, 'The choice is yours, *Meine deutschen Freunde*,' the men looked at him attentively and he noticed the bloodshot eyes and the stress in their faces. They looked like shit. 'Tell me everything and I'll return you to the road and you can go back to wherever it is you are staying. Or my friend and I will beat the information out of you and it will be extremely painful.' Radford was standing by him and Paul could see the Germans' eyes switch to him. He held a canteen of water. 'Let them drink, Barry,' Paul said, 'I believe they want to talk.'

And they did. The smaller man, the leader of the two, told it all. His English was precise and clipped in that typical Germanic manner. 'We work for Frau Hollern. We have come here from Berlin,' and Paul's senses alarmed at this. Would he never shake off the shadow of Berlin? The man continued. 'We only do the hard work for her. You understand what I mean?'

'I do,' he replied. 'Tell me about Frau Hollern.' Paul had an ominous feeling. He turned to Radford and sent the message with his expression: We let them talk then *we* talk later, but *not* in front of these two goons. Radford nodded his head slowly in acknowledgment.

'Frau Hollern runs many businesses in Berlin in the West and the East,' the German continued. 'She only said to come here to England to find a woman. It was for some days, not a long time.'

'Who was the woman, and did you find her?'

'We have her name and how she was described to us and we were told her house location. Yes, we found her.'

'And you broke into her house,' said Paul in a flat statement. Why was that?'

The German instantly looked worried and started to fidget. 'Frau Hollern gave us instructions to search for a handcase or a bag, but,' he went on hastily, 'we found nothing like that.'

'How could it be possible,' the other German suddenly chimed in, 'the place was disorganized. There was nothing there we were looking for.'

Paul resisted the temptation to look at Radford. Of course they had found nothing! 'How is Frau Hollern called? And who is her husband?' This was the crunch. This would bring everything together if his hunch was correct.

'Karin is her given name, and her man is a senior person in *Stern* magazine. You have heard of it?'

Paul nodded his head thoughtfully. His mind was putting the pieces of information in place, joining the dots and the picture emerging was clear. He was certain of it. This time he glanced at Radford, whose face was now animated. Yes, Paul thought, Barry's made the connection as well, because he's done the research I asked him to. 'Where is this woman Frau Karin Hollern now? Here, or close?'

'*Ja*,' said the German. 'We stay on this island of Portland in a castle hotel. It is called Pennsylvania or something like this.'

'When are you leaving?'

'Soon. But first we had to find this case or the woman again. But I think the woman has gone and you have come and so it is now uncertain.'

'You're damned right it is now uncertain,' said Paul. 'Barry, old friend, tape their mouths again and let's get them strapped back in the Rover. We need to talk.'

19

GHOSTS OF BERLIN

'IT'S FIELD'S FIRST wife,' said Barry Radford to Paul. 'Has to be.' The two of them had re-incarcerated the Germans and walked fifty paces away from the vehicle.

Paul felt the heat of the mid-afternoon sun beating down almost directly overhead and forced his system to relax and his mind to think clearly. He had to get this end-piece right. Everything was balanced finely and if he buggered it up then neither Victoria nor Nikki's lives might be quite the same again. Nor his or Radford's for that matter.

Radford spoke quietly but insistently. 'I found the data, Paul, in Poole library, it was all on microfiche. Damn nearly ruined my eyes squinting at the old newspaper cuttings and stories from the sixties and seventies. And it was a rush. He was some bloody crook your Brian Field or Carlton or whatever the hell his name was.' Paul let Radford talk on. It was good to listen to another perspective and he trusted his friend's judgement. 'And it looks as if his ex-wife was the same.'

'What makes you say that?' Paul asked innocuously.

'Well if you read all the material it's pretty clear she was a crook as well and harboured a deep sense of injustice at what happened after the Great Train Robbery.'

'Go on, Barry.' This was a new angle to Paul. Victoria Walker-Haig had obviously not known anything about Brian Carlton's past, or a first wife. Billy Hopkins had told him that Brian Field had a wife at the time of the robbery but had given him little more. No real detail.

'Well, from what I found out, Field and his wife worked a criminal scam from before the time of the Great Train Robbery,' Radford looked seriously at Paul. The quarry was very quiet and very hot. It was a weird setting, a semi-submerged stone world with the desert-like heat bouncing off the rough stone features. The Germans would be cooking in the back of the vehicle. Serves the bastards right, Paul thought.

Radford spoke again. 'The two of them lived high on the hoof and yet he was only a solicitor's clerk and she was an occasional children's nanny, but,' and Radford paused for effect, 'with well-to-do families.'

'So what?' Paul asked, already suspecting he knew the answers.

'Field drove a Jag, apparently, and he worked for a poxy little firm of solicitors. His boss's car was a shag heap. Field and Karin had a house called "Kabri", which is an amalgam of their names, in a place called Whitchurch Hill in Oxfordshire, and how poncey is that? And whilst the same boss lived in a dump of an area? There was also some speculation in the press at the time that the two of them owned another house down in Cornwall. So how?' Radford asked rhetorically. 'Because Field and Karin supplemented their meagre earnings through criminal activity. That's how, I guess.'

'In what way?' Paul asked.

'Amongst other possibly nefarious connections Field had a prior relationship with two of the Great Train Robbers, Buster Edwards and Gordon Goody.' Paul remembered Billy Hopkins' words: *Brian Field had arranged legal representation for Goody and Edwards after their arrest in connection with the Heathrow Airport heist.* 'And apparently Karin would scout out rich houses where she worked as a nanny,' Radford went on, 'and Field would pass on the detail to Edwards and Goody and probably others. The places would then get done over and Field and his wife would receive a sizeable back-hander. How could the couple's inappropriate wealth be explained otherwise?'

'It's hard to argue against,' said Paul. 'What else did you find out about the wife, this woman Karin, who appears to be bloody well here, now, against the odds of all that's believable?'

'She felt cheated by her husband. Plain and simple. She'd been in on all the planning from the outset, had a part to play in the aftermath, knew all the players, expected to get her share of the cash through her husband, saw him go to prison and got nothing as a result. She divorced him sometime between nineteen sixty-four and seven and buggered off back to Germany where she wrote all about it in various magazines, including *Stern.*' He continued, 'And if what those two krauts tell us is true, she married a Mr Hollern who seems to work for the journal in question.'

'You're right, Barry,' Paul said. 'You must be.'

It was getting too hot to be standing still talking and doing nothing. Paul checked his watch. It was almost four o'clock. He wanted to get to the showdown but he had a problem. Since Radford had arrived there hadn't been a moment for Paul to tell his friend the real reasons why he'd been called in to help. Radford had come on trust via an obscure mission to look up some old newspaper information on the woman they both now knew was geographically close to them.

Paul hadn't told him about Nikki and her sister Victoria, or about *why* the Germans were bound and gagged and baking their brains out in the back of his vehicle. He hadn't told Radford about the money! Was he going to? Paul hadn't actually decided; everything since he'd found the blasted cache had happened too quickly. He didn't yet really know what the bastard hell he was going to do with Brian Field's attaché case. He had an idea but it was still a fantastic long shot and depended on so many other things. He was momentarily pondering all this when Radford's next words avalanched him.

'Somehow ex-Mrs Karin Field, now known as Frau Karin Hollern, has come to this place with two henchmen. So why, Paul? Tell me why, old mate? Who's the woman they've been looking for and what's this bloody handcase the kraut was talking about?' Radford looked seriously at Paul. 'If you want me to continue to break the law and beat the shit out of two visitors to these lands, then I need some more info. It's money, isn't it? The mad German bitch has followed the money, hasn't she? And what's it got to do with you? Is it the woman? It must be. For God's sake, Paul, tell me all.'

'You're right about almost everything, Barry. I'll tell you.' Paul sat down on some rocks in the shade of a large overhang. 'But this will be the concise version, because we don't want those krauts dying of natural causes. So get your planet-sized brain around all this and then we'll make the final plan.'

And Paul told Barry Radford the story of The Great Train Robber and how he'd become involved through Nikki and her sister.

'Fuck!' Was the sum total of Radford's comments when Paul stopped.

'And I found the money this morning,' Paul said by way of an ending. 'In the attaché case exactly as Victoria had described it to me. Buried in an old sports bag full of kit and under a mountain of shit and rubbish in the corner of her loft space.'

'Christ, Paul! What a brilliant story!' Radford had been sitting next to Paul for the past few minutes and now stood up. 'Clever bitch, Mrs Field or Frau Hollern,' said Radford, 'and after all these years, too. Must have taken a shedload of investigative resource to track down what she could only have suspected still existed, and to trace it to Victoria and to where she lives now. They must have watched her on and off for a while, mate. Scary thoughts, Paul.'

'Yes. Not nice. These people need to be dealt with.'

'You know what they say, Paul?'

'A woman scorned and all that?'

'Exactly.' Radford looked hard at Paul. 'This woman of yours, the sister Nikki, she's the real thing, eh, Paul?'

'She is and I'm going to protect her at all costs. And her bloody sister, to whom I'm now duty bound.'

'Yes. I agree. So these fucking Germans do need to be dealt with. You know we *are* going to need my Dad's help after all. Aren't we? Think about it.'

Radford was right, thought Paul, but before they called upon the professional and legal help of Chief Superintendant Horace Radford, MBE, of the Metropolitan Police's Serious Crime Squad, they had to finish up here - on their own.

'Maybe we'll need your Dad's help,' said Paul. 'Probably, in fact. But first let's go and talk to Karin Hollern and get this thing finished with. I have the feeling that the best approach is to tell her the money exists but that it's worthless to her and she's not getting it anyway. What do you think?'

Radford laughed. 'It might be, Paul, it just might. You do have a way of being ever so persuasive! But you need a Plan B as well.'

'Which I don't have yet, but it'll come to me. Anyway, time to move. You know the Pennsylvania Castle don't you?'

'Yes. So we don't drop these bastard krauts over the cliff just yet then? Pity, we could bury them without trace here, no problem. But if we did we wouldn't be able to call on Dad for support. Catch-22.'

'No extreme violence just yet, Barry.' Not at all, thought Paul. Too bloody difficult. Too many potential repercussions. And he *was* going to need Police help to finish this thing off, he just knew it. 'There has to be another way. Let's find it.'

So Paul, Radford and the two Germans went to the hotel where Brian Field's first wife waited. They went in search of her and of a reasonable way to finish things.

* * *

BARRY RADFORD PARKED the Land Rover away from the entrance of the hotel in the shade of a huge chestnut tree. The Pennsylvania Castle Hotel looked exactly as it should: like a castle, built of the solid stone of Portland. It had low turrets, paved courtyards, walled gardens and car parks, which were not very full of cars. Its location was isolated. Sightseeing from here required a car.

'There's a terrace, Paul,' stated Radford. 'It has a magnificent view over the sea as far as France. It also drops sheer down onto the rocks. A hundred feet if it's an inch, mate. Bet that's where you'll find her. She'll be sipping a margarita and waiting for her foot soldiers to return reporting success.' Radford was chirpy and animated. 'Look for her there.' He was in all probability right. So Paul didn't even bother with Reception - he went straight outside to the terrace.

And found her.

Billy Hopkins had said that Karin Field was a lovely looker, a right tough woman, to use his own words. And if Paul's experience of smart, professional, ambitious German women was of any consequence, then she would still be a looker. He'd calculated that she could be anything from late forties to early fifties. Field was twenty-eight at the time of the Great Train Robbery and his wife would probably have been of similar age, maybe a little younger.

She was unmistakable.

It was early for sundowners. Too hot. Everyone else was still out and about at the beach or sightseeing. There was only one other, younger couple, at a table further along the terrace. Karin Hollern was on her own, sitting back sipping a cool drink and looking out over the magnificent late afternoon seascape. The drink didn't look like a margarita.

'Frau Hollern?' Paul asked, coming up behind her chair. The woman turned around and took off her sunglasses and then turned back as Paul moved to stand between her and the terrace edge. He could see everything and everyone from here. Although surprised, the woman quickly recovered her composure. Her eyes caught the sun and were strikingly blue. Her hair was short, very blond and stylishly cut. She looked very German, slim and fit. Paul noticed this without her having stood up. Her face was sculpted and pretty, but her lips were thin and gave her demeanour a cold finish. Hmm, he thought.

'Who are you? And how do you know my name?' Her voice was firm and her English almost flawless - well it was likely to be, Paul surmised - but a hint of the Teutonic accent was discernible.

A waiter appeared from the hotel end of the terrace, a tray in his hand and an enquiring look on his face. Paul politely waved him away. The man went inside and Paul turned back to Karin Hollern. 'I'm Major Paul Stanton,' he said, 'and I would like you to come with me, please. There are matters we need to discuss.'

'I do not think so, thank you,' she replied calmly, but Paul picked up just the tiniest hint of uncertainty in her eyes. 'I do not know you or anything about you,' she continued. 'If you do not leave me alone I shall call the hotel management. I am a guest here and waiting for my husband to come down to join me.'

'No, Mrs Field, or ex-Mrs Field, I should say,' and now her face registered genuine flickers of worry, 'I don't believe you will call the authorities. I think you'll come with me, at least to talk,' said Paul with as much mental persuasion he could transmit without scaring her off. 'I believe it would be in your interests, Frau Hollern, not least because my friend and I have both your colleagues in our vehicle outside and they have already told me all about you.' The woman looked uneasily to her left and right. 'If you need to leave a message for your husband, who I believe may still work for *Stern* magazine, if indeed he is even here in England, then you can do it later.' Paul moved around to her chair and pulled it gently backwards. Karin Hollern stood up reluctantly. 'We're only going as far as the car park,' said Paul soothingly.

'I do not like this,' protested the woman, although she picked up her shoulder bag from the terrace and let Paul chaperone her outside, which he did by walking close and just behind her. She wore stylish cotton summer trousers and a loose blouse, but was tall and lithe and would fight hard if she had to, Paul guessed. He did not want to hurt her in any way,

215

though. He abhorred the idea of physical violence involving women. Paul put a smile on his face and continued to talk quietly.

'The mission you set yourself has changed. You cannot continue to do what you have been doing.'

They had reached the outside door of the hotel. She turned an angry face to Paul. 'I know nothing of what you are talking about.'

'Yes you do.' Paul gently nudged her. 'Keep walking, please. You know exactly what I'm talking about. Here we are.' Radford had moved a few paces from the parked Land Rover and come towards them but they were still sheltered by the great branches of the chestnut tree and it was suddenly refreshingly cool. 'This is my friend and colleague, Barry, and you do not need to know anything more about him except that he is a good man and believes in truth and fairness, as I do.' Radford smiled a huge smile and ushered her towards the back of the Rover.

Paul was certain that Radford's physical presence would contribute significantly to the undermining of Karin Hollern's resolve, which was what he had to achieve, and without too much more violence. The woman had to abandon her mission. He would use physical force only as a last resort. He was pretty sure he'd have to threaten it, and in a manner that would be a real deterrent. Not likely to be easy with a woman like Karin Hollern, a woman so clearly steeped in criminal activity.

Radford spoke jauntily, 'There they are, Frau Hollern, your two lovely boys; but I have to tell you, they have not been very good foot soldiers on your behalf,' and he chuckled. When Karin Hollern looked into the back of the Land Rover, her face visibly blanched and her body went tense. Paul stood beside her. She was staring at her two Germans, one on either side of the vehicle, lashed with cargo straps to the iron support struts for the rear canopy, duct tape across their mouths and their feet and hands plasticuffed. The men looked war-battered, dishevelled and wasted. Her upper body sagged and she turned to Paul. He pre-empted her.

'Cut them loose, Barry.'

'Roger that, boss.'

Paul gently turned the woman away from the back of the vehicle. 'I will use physical force again only as a last resort, Frau Hollern, but I have to tell you that my friend and I are very, very good at it. Do you understand me?' She nodded her head and her eyes had lost a touch of their hardness.

'We shall go for a short walk now, and I'll tell you a story and you can tell me a story and then we will agree that you will go back to Berlin and never do this sort of thing again.' Paul looked back at what was happening. The two Germans were standing shakily by the rear of the vehicle. 'Talk to your colleagues, Frau Hollern, and tell them they are free to go. Tell them also that if I ever see them again near this place or me, or anyone who is a friend of mine, then I shall kill them and send their bodies back in boxes to Berlin. Tell them that, please.'

Which Karin Hollern did.

* * *

THE PATHWAY WAS rugged and sloped steeply downwards towards the rocky cove below. Radford followed behind Paul and Karin Hollern. 'There's a footpath down to the sea, Paul,' he'd said when asked. 'It's just off the Church Ope Road, which is right there,' and Radford pointed to the old church sitting in its small grounds next to the Pennsylvania Castle Hotel.

They walked for a few minutes until they reached a stone bench that looked out to sea and from where the rugged coastline of Portland could be viewed.

'Please sit, Frau Hollern,' Paul said and the woman sat. Barry Radford stood close behind listening but on the lookout. 'Let me start the story I said we were both going to tell.' It was still very hot and there was plenty of daylight left in the day but Paul didn't want to tarry too long. However, there was an important part of the deterrent process to be established. He had thought about this as they'd walked and concluded that as a woman of Berlin, with all her history and connections, Karin Hollern would have heard about Otto Krenselauer.

'I do not know what you expect from me, but I have nothing to say to you. I have no story for you.' It was the first time Karin Hollern had spoken since she'd admonished her two men and sent them back into the hotel. With his smattering of German Paul had understood what she'd said to them: she had told them of his threat to their future wellbeing and also to be ready to leave - soon. Which was good, he'd thought, at least she's not thinking of making a fighting stand - well not here.

Paul ignored her riposte. 'You were in Berlin three years ago?'

'Yes. Of course. I have been there for many years, it is where I live.'

'Yes it is. Good. And you are a business woman and you are married to a respected journalist who works for *Stern*, so you will have heard at that time of the arrest of Otto Krenselauer.'

'No. I do not know of anyone of that name.'

'I don't believe you.' The Krenselauer arrest had been a cause célèbre in the Western papers at the time. Paul went on, 'Otto Krenselauer was a notorious quartermaster for the Red Army Faction in Berlin. He was a fanatical supporter and confidant of Ulrike Meinhof. After her death he went on a terror spree and was responsible for the kidnappings and murders in late nineteen seventy-seven, that you Germans called *Der Deutsche Herbst*, the German Autumn. It was period of extreme violence, disruption and terror.' Paul was watching the woman closely and knew from her eyes and facial twitches she knew exactly what he was talking about. 'Then Krenselauer just disappeared. Until nineteen eighty-six.'

'Who was this guy, Paul?' said Radford, who was watching and listening. Karin Hollern looked at him in surprise, as if she'd forgotten he was there.

'He was a fat, murdering, evil little shit of a man, who had appalling taste in décor and cigarettes, so I'm told, and who ran a number of black market, illegal, cross-Berlin businesses that included the sale of raw pornography and military intelligence.'

'Christ, Paul, how do you know this?'

Karin Hollern had stiffened in her body and was watching Paul intently. Paul looked directly at her. He was taking a bit of risk concerning his personal security but reckoned it was worth it and that given her own history, Karin Hollern would be discrete with what he told her.

So he said, 'Because I was responsible for his arrest by the Berlin and Federal German authorities in nineteen eighty-six, and because I killed his business associates in Berlin,' which wasn't totally true, Paul acknowledged to himself; but he had killed one of them, as well as the British Army corporal who'd been trading military information with Krenselauer. But the other Krenselauer thug had shot Paul and damn nearly killed him. Thankfully his partner in undercover ops at the time, Corporal Troy Halliday of the Scottish Infantry, had been there to save his life. Karin Hollern didn't need *that* amount of detail.

'Fucking hell,' said Radford. 'So that's what all that furore in Berlin was about!' He spoke to Karin Hollern. 'You need to respect all this heavy stuff, Frau Hollern. I've seen some action in my time, but this man, Stanton, is something else when it comes to the black operations world.'

'Anyway,' said Paul. 'Let me continue by changing the subject and talking about the Great Train Robbery,' at which Karin Hollern swivelled around from looking at Radford to stare once more at Paul.

'What!' she exclaimed.

'Well, more specifically,' said Paul, 'your ex-husband's share of the money from the Great Train Robbery.' Paul had decided he would go straight for the jugular, and he had the woman's full attention now. Her eyes were big and her face taut. 'Brian Field was sentenced to thirty years. You divorced him whilst he was in prison. You didn't wait for his appeal to be lodged. If you had, you wouldn't really have had to wait too long for your man to be released, because his sentence was reduced to five years.' The woman's attention was obvious. She was gripped. 'But you'd divorced him and subsequently wrote some articles in *Stern* in which you admitted close involvement in the pre- and post-Robbery activity. You remarried, a journalist of some repute who supplied articles and copy pieces for various papers and magazines including *Stern*.'

Paul paused, but the woman said nothing. He went on. 'You were already a minor criminal,' and the woman raised her eyebrows at this statement but still said nothing, 'and you were complicit in the planning and preparation for the Robbery. Brian Field provided the initial contact with the so-called Ulsterman, who gave the vital information on the train and the banknotes, and his law firm made the purchase of Leatherslade Farm to be used by the robbers after the heist. You knew everyone involved, you hosted a post-robbery piss up at your house, Kabri, but,' and Paul paused and then deliberately emphasized the words, '*you never got your share of the money*. And after your ex-husband's release from prison he deliberately chose *never* to give you anything.'

'It is not so.'

'Yes it is. He changed his name and his life.' Paul looked closely at her. 'But you found out about him, didn't you?'

Paul's words seemed to break down the woman's last defences. Her body visibly crumpled for a few seconds but then she took a deep breath and sat upright, fixing him with hard eyes.

'How you know all this, I am not sure, but a lot of what you say is correct. And as you have me at a disadvantage and it is clear that I am in the company of two killer-men, I will tell you the truth.'

'Make sure it is the truth, Frau Hollern, and then if we can make an agreement you can go.'

The woman shuddered and spoke. 'I was always involved in whatever Brian did. I told this in the articles I wrote in Germany after the robbery. I knew them all, the main men. Gordon Goody stayed at our house before the job. It was our friend Mark who was to help with the clean up of the farm. But the plans had to change and they all had to leave the farm earlier than they thought. So it was Brian, me and Mark who helped Bruce Reynolds and the others to get cars and who brought the vans from the farm and drove the rest of the men to our house.' She looked suddenly wistful for a moment as she went on. 'We had a wonderful party that Friday night. We were young and carefree then and had just carried out the biggest cash robbery in history! Then it all went wrong,' and the unemotional sternness returned to her tone. 'Everyone split and four days later Brian had to go to London because Bruce

Reynolds, Charlie Wilson and Buster Edwards wanted reassurance that there was no evidence left at the farm.'

'But there was, wasn't there?' chimed in Radford. 'You see, Frau Hollern, we've done our research.'

'Yes. And it was the beginning of the end of course. Did you know Brian was almost killed by Wilson at that meeting in London? And the next day the news said that the Police had discovered the farm. When Brian came back home I could see the change in him. He was frightened; and he started to act secretively and to exclude me from his thoughts.' She looked at Paul, as if seeking his sympathy. 'We always, always agreed we would share everything, but Brian gave me nothing, *nichts. Das Geld verschwunden.*'

'Where do you think the money went?' Paul asked.

'Brian hid it,' she replied, without hesitation. 'He used some of it to hire a brilliant lawyer, let some of it be discovered and then collected it all later when he got out of prison. He was a very clever man.' Paul and Radford exchanged glances. 'And he had more than his own share of the cut,' Karin Hollern stood up and faced Paul. 'He had the share for the Ulsterman and also for Mark.' She looked at Radford. 'That was a very large amount of money.'

'And you believe this money still exists somewhere?' said Paul cautiously. 'How can that be so, given that Brian Field died ten years ago and before that he had been living another life since nineteen sixty-seven? And why are you here, in this place, looking for a particular woman?'

'I do believe it. I always believed Brian had a plan for after he was released from prison. I always believed he had let

223

some of the money be found to leave a false trail. My husband and I have carried out a great deal of research and we are sure we know Brian's story after he was released.'

'Please tell me why you are here, Frau Hollern?' Paul was beginning to get impatient. This situation needed to be crystallized. He felt the distractions of the Great Train Robbery story pulling him away from the two huge problems that still remained to be resolved: how to get rid of this woman forever; and what to do with the money.

'It is simple, *Major* Stanton,' she'd remembered his name, thought Paul, which was good because he wanted her to. 'I would like my share of Brian's money.' And in a glimpse of things not already seen, Paul realized that Karin Hollern was totally obsessed and probably slightly mad.

'Are you crazy?' he asked seriously. 'If the money still existed and you got your hands on it, how would you be able to use it? Did you see the money after the robbery? Even if you didn't, you know it was all in used five and one pound banknotes, banknotes of nineteen sixty-three vintage which you could never, never use today!'

'I would find a way. It has some value to certain people. And I was always to have my share.' Yes, Paul thought, she's obsessed to the point of slight madness. Then Karin Hollern said something that made him re-think his assessment of her. 'Besides, Brian was clever and he would have changed the money and be living on it. Yes, he was very clever.'

Paul steered Karin Hollern away from this theme. 'Why are you here?'

'We found Brian with his new identity and new wife some years after his time in prison. We knew where he was living in London. We knew he was living in the same house as another woman who worked for him.'

'Did you watch this house in London and then try to break in and steal something?' Paul asked. He had a feeling.

'Yes,' she said and looked at him with serious surprise. 'How do you know this and why do you ask?'

'Go on, Frau Hollern, tell me what happened in London.'

'We stole a suitcase before Christmas one year but there was nothing in it, only a woman's clothes. Then we lost sight of this woman for some time but we still watched Brian and his new wife. Until,' and Karin Hollern looked momentarily sad, 'he was no longer there, at that house in London, in Kew.'

'Because he was killed in a car crash,' said Radford.

'We did not discover this until some weeks later, of course,' said Karin Hollern. 'By this time the woman who was his friend had disappeared. We never found her again until eventually we could track her movements through the estate agents that sold her property. It was many years before we had any idea where she had moved to.'

It was, thought Paul, ten years or thereabouts. And it was exactly as Victoria Walker-Haig had told him. She'd spent the first two years bar bumming in the Canaries and then sold her flat in Kew and come down to Weymouth and Portland to start a new career. She'd been overseas when Brian Carlton and his wife Sian had been killed.

'We found she moved to this area,' continued Karin Hollern, 'and according to our research and enquiries she is the last remaining person to have had contact with Brian at the time when he was killed in that car crash.'

'So what, exactly,' Paul asked guilelessly, 'do you think it all means?'

'It means that if anyone had Brian's money or knew where it was, then she would.'

'Not necessarily, Frau Hollern, not at all.' And in this moment Paul decided that Plan A was what he was going with and there would be no Plan B. He looked at Radford and motioned him to come and stand next to him. He wanted the German woman to see exactly who and what she was dealing with. 'What you say is not so, and you really do need to change your mind about this, or it will bring you pain and big trouble with the authorities in this country.'

'How so, Herr *Major*?'

'Because I know this woman you speak of. Why do you think we are talking to you now and why do you think my colleague, Barry, is also with me?' Karin Hollern shrugged and tried to appear nonchalant. It didn't work. The woman was slipping out of her depth. Paul could read the uncertainty in her eyes and the tightness around her mouth. 'The woman is a good friend of mine,' he continued. 'You and your thugs have scared her. She came to me and talked about all these things. She is not a stupid woman and she knows that Brian Carlton is the reason why she is being terrorized by you.'

'So you know then that I must be right.'

'No,' replied Paul, 'quite the opposite. My friend has told me things that you do not to know.'

'What things?' Karin Hollern asked.

'My friend *never*,' and Paul emphasised the word, 'knew Brian Carlton was Brian Field the Great Train Robber. Never. She told me this and I believe her. Brian Carlton was a man she met in the local pub, discovered was a neighbour and who offered her a job. She simply worked for him and became a friend of his wife, and only for a short period.'

'I don't believe this.'

'At the time your ex-husband and his wife were killed,' Paul continued, ignoring her interjection, 'my friend had already stopped working for Brian. Shortly before that weekend, Brian's wife was talking to my friend and telling her that she had to put something into a safety deposit box at a bank for security before they went away.' Karin Hollern's face perked up and she studied Paul intently. 'It was obviously something valuable.' Paul looked at Radford and raised his eyebrows.

'The money,' said Radford, 'or at least whatever our Robber had turned the money into. And then they were killed. Tragedy.'

'My friend had gone overseas by then,' continued Paul, 'and did not hear about the accident or the fact of Carlton's true identity until many weeks later whilst she was still abroad.'

'And from the research we've done,' said Radford, 'Brian Carlton-Field had no next of kin. How could he? No one knew who he was! So it seems like the last laugh might be on you, Frau Hollern, with Brian's horde, if that's what it was, locked in some unknown safety deposit box forever.' Radford smiled broadly. 'Come on Paul, let's get away from this crazy scene.'

'In a minute, Barry,' Paul acknowledged his friend's impatience. He felt it himself. 'There's one final thing to say.' Karin Hollern's body stiffened. 'You committed another crime by ordering your thugs to watch and frighten my friend and then to break into her home and smash it up.' The look on the woman's face was anticipatory. 'The crime,' Paul said, 'I'd never be able to prove. But you have terrorized a woman, my friend, and violated the sanctity of her personal property and belongings and in this you have crossed a line.' The German woman made to speak but Paul put his hand up to shush her. 'So you will leave tomorrow morning, on the ferry from Weymouth, you and your two men, and you will never come back here again. Do you understand me?'

'Yes,' the woman replied, faintly. Her eyes were huge and her face held fear and worry in its lines. Paul was angry now and he moved and stood over her. His presence was foreboding and his anger palpable. Radford made to put a hand of restraint out towards his friend, then withdrew it as Paul spoke again.

'Go back to Berlin, Frau Hollern. Tell your husband your investigations are over. The Great Train Robber is long dead and his money is long gone and where it belonged, back in a bank somewhere. And remember this: there are ghosts I have left in Berlin and if I have to I shall come there again and make more ghosts. If I have to I shall come and find you and those dear to you and cause you very great pain. It is what I do, Frau Hollern.' Paul took a deep breath and turned to Radford, 'I'm done, Barry, let's get out of this place.'

'Roger that, Paul.'

'I shall be at the ferry terminal tomorrow morning, Frau Hollern. You'll see me and I shall wave goodbye to you and your men. Forever.'

And with that Paul and Radford left the German woman and walked back up the rock footpath and into the normality of a beautiful late afternoon in Dorset.

20

JUST REWARDS?

THEY WERE IN Victoria Walker-Haig's cottage, relaxing in her back sitting-dining room away from prying eyes and with the front door locked and curtains drawn, sipping whisky. Radford had insisted on a fish supper. Paul had brought the attaché case in from his car. It stood in its battered, old-fashioned form on the floor in front of the two men. He needed to examine it and then…well, he'd decide in a few minutes, hopefully.

Paul told Radford his intentions. 'I'm opening the case, Barry, and then I'm going to make the decision on what I do.'

'Go for it, Paul, it's your shout, my friend. I've got some picklocks if you'd like. Don't want to bugger up the package too much, do we?' And he laughed and went and fetched the tools from the gear he'd dumped in the front room. 'Know how to use these?' Radford said, handing Paul his picklocks. 'You'd better put these on, mate,' he continued, offering a pair of rubber gloves. 'Don't want to be leaving any fingerprints.'

'Thanks. You're right.' Paul took the picklocks and put on the gloves. Now he'd been forced by Karin Hollern's stance into a course of action, he was determined on seeing it through, but it reeked of potential disaster. He needed to see exactly what he was dealing with.

'Christ almighty!' Radford spoke first, as the locks on the flap of the attaché case were opened for the first time in over ten years and the two of them peered inside. Paul said nothing as he struggled to wrap his mind around his first impressions. 'Lay it all out, Paul, on the table behind us, come on. Have you ever seen anything like this?'

Paul hadn't.

The attaché case could only have measured eighteen inches by twelve, but when freed from its clasp locks - which had been ridiculously simple to pick - it opened to reveal two deep compartments and smelt musty. One compartment held a number of velvet bags, each tied at the neck with a ribbon. Diamonds. They had to be. Or gemstones. And on top of these small bags were banded bundles of new-looking bank notes. The other compartment was stacked full of gold coins.

'Wow,' Paul said, finally. 'Hmm, I'm going to have to think this through. Let's see what we have, Barry, but memorise how it's all packed in here, OK?'

Neither Paul nor Barry knew it yet but Brian Field had amassed a horde of high denomination Swiss Franc banknotes and wallets of one-ounce gold bullion coins including South African Krugerrands, Austrian Philharmoniker and 100 Coronas, British Sovereigns and of all things Chinese Gold Pandas. There were twenty small velvet bags of diamonds - twenty!

Over the years since his release from prison, Brian Field had clearly traded the old, laundered Great Train Robbery cash and newer earned and misappropriated cash for hard assets, in the diamond markets in Holland and Switzerland and the bullion markets in the European capital cities he'd visited regularly. And he'd probably done all this whilst working for the Children's Book Centre. What a bastard! But he'd been generous and kind to Victoria Walker-Haig so he couldn't have been all bad.

'So what's the plan then, Major Stanton?'

'Good question, Major Radford.' But Paul knew what his plan was, he'd decided on it very quickly and easily once he'd seen inside the case. 'I think I'm going to steal some of the gold and give it to good causes.'

'You are kidding me, aren't you?'

'No. No kidding. That's exactly what I'm going to do. Who's going to miss it? Who, apart from us and Nikki and her sister even knows this horde actually exists? And Victoria doesn't really have a clue.'

'Good causes?' said Radford. 'What are you, Paul, some kind of modern-day Robin Hood?'

'I think I am - in this case!' Paul laughed and sipped from his glass. 'I'm not keeping anything for myself - don't need or want for anything. What about you?'

'Fuck off, Paul! I'm an officer of Her Majesty's Royal Marines and my Dad's a copper! Of course I don't want any of this illicit bung. I might take a handful of those gold bullion coins, mind, for when the old Land Rover packs in and I need a new engine!' And Radford laughed, too. 'Are they easy to exchange for hard cash?'

'I don't actually know, but I would think they are. It's all untraceable, Barry.'

'I'm joking! Don't let the stuff anywhere near me. You know how weak willed I am in the company of beautiful ladies. So what are the good causes?'

'Victoria and her sister, Nikki.'

'I like that. How much?'

'Not a huge amount and it won't be missed. There's over two million pounds here.'

'What! How do you know?'

'I don't actually but I'm guessing based on the fact that Brian Field's residual cash from his and the other shares from the Robbery, in today's values are approximately two million if they're in hard assets, which clearly they are. I had Nikki check out the inflation equations with friends of hers in the City.'

'Where does the rest come from? Field or Carlton's dodgy dealings later?'

'It must do. When Victoria was telling me her story she mentioned that Carlton and his wife lived a lavish lifestyle, and she talked about one specific incident when all the cash from a big exhibition and sales session abroad was supposedly stolen. I'm pretty sure Carlton was siphoning off cash from the Children's Book Centre and adding it to this horde of goodies.'

'Once a crook always a crook, eh, Paul?'

'Exactly. But what an ironic twist of fate.' Radford cocked his eyebrow. 'Field managed to get away with his share of the Great Train Robbery cash and increase its wealth by cheating everybody,' said Paul, 'but was still cheated of its full benefit in the end because he couldn't cheat death!'

'Fucking tragic, mate. My heart bleeds for the cheating bastard.'

'God got it right for once,' said Paul. 'Shame about his new wife, though. Vikki said she was a lovely person.' Paul counted the number of gold coin wallets and put a quarter of them to one side. He then repacked the remainder in the case, along with the diamonds and banknotes. 'Is that how it all looked?'

'That's it, mate. Now lock that little danger zone up firmly and resist all temptation to commit an even bigger crime than we have all ready!'

Paul did so. 'Good,' he said. 'Now I've got a call to make to a beautiful woman who will be worried about us.'

* * *

'WELL THAT'S THEM gone,' said Radford as the Channel Islands ferry chugged its way out of Weymouth harbour the next morning.

They'd seen Karin Hollern and the two Germans arrive in a taxi and embark. Paul had even shouted out goodbye and waved at them to ensure they knew he was watching them. The woman had taken Paul's warning seriously. He was glad his bluff had not been called.

'What now, mate?' Radford enquired. 'I have to shoot off back to work if you've no further need of me.'

'Now we call your Dad,' replied Paul. 'But we stick to the plan. Agreed. No going back. Can you live with it?'

'Are you joking, my dear friend. Of course I can.'

'Good. And you'll be back in Poole in good time to complete the training week with your boys.'

'Thanks a lot!'

So Barry Radford telephoned his father at The Metropolitan Police Services' Headquarters at New Scotland Yard, made the introduction for Paul and handed him the handset.

Chief Superintendant Horace Radford listened seriously as Paul gave him the snapshot of what had gone on down in Portland and what Paul and Barry had uncovered. Paul was invited to meet him at New Scotland Yard the day after tomorrow; which was good, thought Paul, because Thursday was the day when Nikki was meeting with the MozLon teams to make her pitch for Danny Dalloway's contract in Mozambique, and she would have her mind on other things.

* * *

COULD PAUL STANTON have predicted the outcome of that telephone call? No, is the simple answer, because the outcome never occurred to him. The fact that it made him feel more guilty about siphoning off some of Brian Field's assets for Victoria and Nikki was an unpalatable fact of life, because by then it was too late to change what he had done.

So how did it all end?

Very well, as it happened.

Horace Radford had prepared everything by the time Paul arrived in his office on the Thursday. He had the case files on Brian Field. He had a stenographer ready to take his statement, which he would check later and duly sign, and he had with him a Detective Inspector from the Flying Squad, the unit inside the Met Police that had led the hunt for the Great Train Robbers from the outset.

And he had a reward. Or at least the promise of one.

Paul was a model player. He told the truth, well almost. He reassured Barry's father that his son's role was merely incidental, that he'd needed a trusted friend as witness and helper, and the Chief Superintendant nodded and looked relieved. Paul also kept Victoria Walker-Haig's part to the absolute minimum: she was, he asserted, an innocent bystander. He spilt the beans fully on Karin Hollern, which pricked the interest of the Flying Squad Inspector greatly and provoked a discussion about informing Interpol and ensuring the *Bundespolizei* in Berlin were aware.

Paul did not mention that he had taken a quarter of the gold bullion coins from the attaché case.

The case in question was placed on a side table in splendid isolation and visually scrutinised but not touched. The Flying Squad Inspector used Horace Radford's 'phone and within a few seconds a plain clothes detective came in wearing forensic gloves and took the item away, for evidence and forensic examination, it was explained. Paul thought it was all a bit too late to be evidence, but what did he know of police procedure?

Then Horace Radford spoke. 'That's an amazing story, Paul.' Radford senior looked at his Flying Squad colleague who nodded in sympathy and Paul could see from the look on both their faces that they *really* did believe it was an amazing story! Thank the Lord Barry had remembered the rubber gloves. 'Did you know that there has been a reward in place since nineteen sixty-three for information leading to the recovery of any of the Great Train Robbery cash?' said Horace Radford.

Paul replied that he didn't. Which he hadn't. The thought had never crossed his mind.

'Well there is,' Chief Superintendant Radford said, 'and it's quite sizeable depending on the amount of the stolen money actually recovered.' Paul said nothing. He was on the shore of shark-infested waters here. Keep your balance, Paul, say absolutely nothing, man. Any hint that he knew what was inside the attaché case and he would be shark bait. 'I'll let you know what we find, Major Stanton,' said Barry Radford's father, adding a touch of formality just to bring the proceedings to an agreeable and respectful end.

On his way back to Pimlico, Paul took a diversion and visited a small Jewish goldsmith in one of the City's side streets. He needed information and a means to this particular end; and he wanted to surprise Nikki when she got back from her meetings with MozLon.

As it turned out the meetings had been a huge success and the Company had virtually committed themselves to awarding the Mozambique deal to Danny Dalloway's Gurkha Connections Limited, pending a few final formalities, nothing serious. So Paul and Nikki had gone out and celebrated with some champagne.

Once back in the flat in Pimlico Paul had presented her with his news.

'I'll shortly have a present for you, Nik.'

'Shortly?' Nikki questioned, jokingly. 'What kind of present is that, Stanton? I'll only accept it if it's huge and sparkles and fits on my finger,' she said laughingly and hugged him hard. 'Does it?'

'No…it could do, but I'll have to talk to you about that later.' Paul was momentarily stumped by her candidness. 'It's actually going to be something in the region of fifty thousand pounds.' Paul watched the amazement grow on her face. 'I thought it might buy you a flat, or something. If you want to, that is.'

'*If I want to!* You naughty man, Stanton, you'd better come here and tell me all about this life-changing present. Is it legal?'

'Of course it is. And there will be the same for Victoria.'

* * *

NIKKI HAD RETURNED to Kathmandu by the time Paul Stanton received news of the amount of the reward. Fifty thousand pounds, said Chief Superintendant Horace Radford. The amount of bullion, gemstones and cash in Brain Field's attaché case had been far in excess of what was thought possible. The reward was legal, non-taxable and would be paid to him by a Bankers Draft. Should it be sent to the Ministry of Defence? Yes, Paul told him, that would be excellent.

Fifty thousand pounds! How could that be? What an outcome, Paul reflected in amazement.

The story of Brian Field, The Great Train Robber, was finally at an end.

Who says crime never pays?

THE NOVEL

Friends In Need is actually two separately written novellas, which I have revised and joined together in the two parts of what is now the second Paul Stanton novel. Those readers who feel this is a bit of a cheat may have a point. However, there is a defence for my action and to me it seems to make sense.

When I created Paul Stanton as a modern-day, slightly understated action hero, I set out to achieve two things: first to involve him as a conventional and an undercover military man in certain incidents in the decade 1985 to 1995; and secondly, whilst doing this, to draw on his experiences with the Scottish Infantry, the Gurkhas and of course the SAS, to show the type of person and soldier he was.

Why did I choose these ten years? And has the correlation with Stanton's experiences worked? Well yes, and no. Let me explain briefly.

The decade 1985-1995 was a fascinating period for politico-military events in which someone like Paul Stanton could become involved in both conventional and deniable operations on behalf of Her Majesty's Government. For a start, he was a soldier in Northern Ireland, and there was a big story to be told there, as well as some myths to debunk about the Long War. The decade also witnessed the beginning of the end of repressionist regimes such as those in Eastern Europe with the fall of the Berlin Wall, and in South Africa with the ending of apartheid. But hot on the heels of these seismic events, the end of the Cold War presaged politico-military interventions in failed states as far afield as the Gulf and the Balkans, where HMG would necessarily become involved. Even further afield, just as South Africa came to recognise the greatness of Nelson Mandela, Mugabe's regime in Zimbabwe was ten years into its systematic wrecking of that bounteous country and other southern African states were still fighting violent civil wars; all of which, in small or large part had some impact on British interests.

So what, you might ask? Well, as I've said, the story of Northern Ireland had to be told, and *The Return* is Paul Stanton's foray in this 'war' as both a conventional Scottish soldier and an SAS man on a deniable operation for HMG. The problem was the Gurkhas.

Stanton served with them in the Far East and they left a profound impression on him. He was, after all, a pretty tough and capable soldier, but with the Gurkhas he saw warrior qualities and skills that were without match, in his experience. Because of the political and military factors already mentioned, and the ideas I had developed for the second Stanton novel, I had always thought to bring Gurkhas into Stanton's exploits in southern Africa, right at the end of the decade in 1989. The story's setting though was unconventional and the presence of Gurkhas in that particular region and time needed to be prefaced in some way. So I had the idea to create the context for this in a short episode set in

Kathmandu in December 1988, whilst Stanton is on leave. This was *The Favour* and it seemed to work fine; but it also introduced a new woman into Stanton's life, a woman who would be a main player in his future exploits in southern Africa.

So far, so good, but then, in the summer of 2013, as I was writing the next novel, and Stanton was there, in London, at Headquarters Director Special Forces, in October 1989, unknowingly on the verge of having his life turned upside down once again, I was told the story of *The Great Train Robber*. 2013 was of course the 50th anniversary of this 'Crime of the Century'. I found the story compelling and immediately began to consider how I could work Stanton into the particular scenario. So I halted Stanton in London, took him back in time three months, gave him some summer leave, allowed him to develop the increasingly vital relationship with his new girl, and used the story to provide additional context for the adventure I had planned for him in southern Africa.

So there it is: the defence for my action in combining the two novellas into this second Paul Stanton novel. The chronology worked, Stanton's experiences with the Scottish Infantry, the Gurkhas and the SAS have been shown to us, *and*, he has a serious romance to lighten his otherwise too-dark soul.

And what about the southern African odyssey? Well *The Contract* will tell this story and I have already written it. And as for Stanton's future involvement in those interventions in failed states I mentioned? I have a mind to send Paul

Stanton on a final mission, and it will most probably be set in the Balkans in 1995, or thereabouts.

THE AUTHOR

Chris Darnell is a retired British Army Colonel and businessman.

He was commissioned in 1971 into the 2nd Gurkha Rifles and later transferred into The King's Own Scottish Borderers. After thirty years of regimental duty all over the world, staff tours in large headquarters in Germany and UK, and too much operational service in Northern Ireland, the Persian Gulf War and the Balkans, he resigned from the Army and worked for global companies in Defence and Technology specialising in the NATO Region.

Now he gives his time to charitable activities, being a Governor of his old school, Haileybury, and writing, amongst other things, Paul Stanton thrillers.

He and his wife live in Weymouth, England and Knysna, South Africa.

Printed in Great Britain
by Amazon